UP IN SMOKE

GLOCK GRANNIES COZY MYSTERY, BOOK 1

SHANNON VANBERGEN

FAIRFIELD PUBLISHING

I COULD FEEL my hair puffing up like cotton candy in the humidity as I stepped outside the Miami airport. I pushed a sticky strand from my face, and I wished for a minute that it were a cheerful pink instead of dirty blond, just to complete the illusion.

"Thank you so much for picking me up from the airport." I smiled at the sprightly old lady I was struggling to keep up with. "But why did you say my grandmother couldn't pick me up?"

"I didn't say." She turned and gave me a toothy grin—clearly none of them original—and winked. "I parked over here."

When we got to her car, she opened the trunk and threw in the sign she had been holding when she met me in baggage claim. The letters were done in gold glitter glue and she had drawn flowers with markers all around the edges. My name "Nikki Rae Parker" flashed when the sun reflected off of them, temporarily blinding me.

"I can tell you put a lot of work into that sign." I carefully put my luggage to the side of it, making sure not to touch her sign—partially because I didn't want to crush it and partially because it didn't look like the glue had dried yet.

"Well, your grandmother didn't give me much time to make it. I only had about ten minutes." She glanced at the sign proudly before closing the trunk. She looked me in the eyes. "Let's get on the road. We can chit chat in the car."

With that, she climbed in and clicked on her seat belt. As I got in, she was applying a thick coat of bright red lipstick while looking in the rearview mirror. "Gotta look sharp in case we get pulled over." She winked again, her heavily wrinkled eyelid looking like it thought about staying closed before it sprung back up again.

I thought about her words for a moment. She must get pulled over a lot, I thought. Poor old lady. I could picture her going ten miles an hour while the rest of Miami flew by her.

"Better buckle up." She pinched her lips together before blotting them slightly on a tissue. She smiled at me and for a moment, I was jealous of her pouty lips, every line filled in by layers and layers of red.

I did as I was told and buckled my seat belt before I sunk down into her caramel leather seats. I was exhausted, both physically and mentally, from the trip. I closed my eyes and tried to forget my troubles, taking in a deep breath and letting it out slowly to give all my worry and fear ample time to escape my body. For the first time since I had made the decision to come here, I felt at peace. Unfortunately, it was short-lived.

The sound of squealing tires filled the air and my eyes flung open to see this old lady zigzagging through the parking garage. She took the turns without hitting the brakes, hugging each curve like a racecar driver. When we exited the garage and turned onto the street, she broke out in laughter. "That's my favorite part!"

I tugged my seat belt to make sure it was on tight. This was not going to be the relaxing drive I had thought it would be.

We hit the highway and I felt like I was in an arcade game. She wove in and out of traffic at a speed I was sure matched her old age.

"Ya know, the older I get the worse other people drive." She took one hand off the wheel and started to rummage through her purse, which sat between us.

"Um, can I help you with something?" My nerves were starting to get the best of me as her eyes were focused more on her purse than the road.

"Oh no, I've got it. I'm sure it's in here somewhere." She dug a little more, pulling out a package of AA batteries and then a ham sandwich.

Brake lights lit up in front of us and I screamed, bracing myself for impact. The old woman glanced up and pulled the car to the left in a quick jerk before returning to her purse. Horns blared from behind us.

"There it is!" She pulled out a package of wintergreen Life Savers. "Do you want one?"

"No, thank you." I could barely get the words out.

"I learned a long time ago that it was easier if I just drove and did my thing instead of worrying about what all the other drivers were doing. It's easier for them to get out of my way instead of me getting out of theirs. My reflexes aren't what they used to be." She popped a mint in her mouth and smiled. "I love wintergreen. I don't know why peppermint is more popular. Peppermint is so stuffy; wintergreen is fun."

She seemed to get in a groove with her driving and soon my grip was loosening on the sides of the seat, the blood slowly returning to my knuckles. Suddenly I realized I hadn't asked her name.

"I was so confused when you picked me up from the airport instead of my Grandma Dean that I never asked your name."

She didn't respond, just kept her eyes on the road with a steely look on her face. I was happy to see her finally being serious about driving, so I turned to look out the window. "It's beautiful here," I said after a few minutes of silence. I turned to look at her again and noticed that she was still focused straight ahead. I stared at her for a moment and realized she never blinked. Panic rose through my chest.

"Ma'am!" I shouted as I leaned forward to take the wheel. "Are you okay?"

She suddenly sprung to action, screaming and jerking the wheel to the left. Her screaming caused me to scream and I grabbed the wheel and pulled it to the right, trying to get us back in our lane. We continued to scream until the car stopped teetering and settled down to a nice hum on the road.

"Are you trying to kill us?" The woman's voice was hoarse and she seemed out of breath.

"I tried to talk to you and you didn't answer!" I practically shouted. "I thought you had a heart attack or something!"

"You almost gave me one!" She flashed me a dirty look. "And you made me swallow my mint. You're lucky I didn't choke to death!"

"I'm sorry." As I said the words, I noticed my heart was beating in my ears. "I really thought something had happened to you."

She was quiet for a moment. "Well, to be honest with you, I did doze off for a moment." She looked at me, pride spreading across her face. "I sleep with my eyes open. Do you know anyone who can do that?"

Before I could answer, she was telling me about her friend Delores who "claimed" she could sleep with her eyes open but, as it turned out, just slept with one eye half-open because she had a stroke and it wouldn't close all the way.

I sat there in silence before saying a quick prayer. My hands resumed their spot around the seat cushion and I could feel the blood draining from my knuckles yet again.

"So what was it you tried to talk to me about before you nearly killed us?"

I swallowed hard, trying to push away the irritation that fought to come out.

"I asked you what your name was." I stared at her and decided right then that I wouldn't take my eyes off of her for the rest of the trip. I would make sure she stayed awake, even if it meant talking to her the entire time.

"Oh yes! My name is Hattie Sue Miller," she said with a bit of arrogance. She glanced at me. "My father used to own most of this land." She motioned to either side of us. "Until he sold it and made a fortune." She gave me a look and dropped her voice to a whisper as she raised one eyebrow. "Of course we don't talk about money. That would be inappropriate." She said that last part like I had just asked her when she had last had sex. I felt ashamed until I realized I had never asked her about her money; I had simply asked her name. This woman was a nut. Didn't Grandma Dean have any other friends she could've sent to get me?

For the next hour or so, I asked her all kinds of questions to keep her awake—none of them about money or anything I thought might lead to money. If what she told me was true, she had a very interesting upbringing. She claimed to be related to Julia Tuttle, the woman who founded Miami. Her stories of how she got a railroad company to agree to build tracks there were fascinating. It wasn't until she told me she was also related to Michael Jackson that I started to question how true her stories were.

"We're almost there! Geraldine will be so happy to see you. You're all she's talked about the last two weeks." She pulled into a street lined with palm trees. "You're going to love it here." She smiled as she drove. "I've lived here a long time. It's far enough away from the city that you don't have all that hullaballoo, but big enough that you can eat at a different restaurant every day for a month."

When we entered the downtown area, heavy gray smoke hung in the air, and the road was blocked by a fire truck and two police cars.

"Oh no! I think there might have been a fire!" I leaned forward in my seat, trying to get a better look.

"Of course there was a fire!" Hattie huffed like I was an idiot. "That's why Geraldine sent me to get you!"

"What?! Is she okay?" I scanned the crowd and saw her immediately. She was easy to spot, even at our distance.

"Oh yes. She's fine. Her shop went up in flames as she was headed out the door. She got the call from a neighboring store owner and called me right away to go get you. Honestly, I barely had time to make you a sign." She acted like Grandma Dean had really put her in a bad position, leaving her only minutes to get my name on a piece of poster board.

Hattie pulled over and I jumped out; I'd come back for my luggage later. As I made my way toward the crowd, I was amazed at how little my Grandma Dean—or Grandma Dean-Dean, as I had called her since I was a little girl—had changed. Her bleach blonde hair was nearly white and cut in a cute bob that was level with her chin. She wore skintight light blue denim capris, which hugged her tiny frame. Her bright white t-shirt was the background for a long colorful necklace that appeared to be a string of beads. Thanks to a pair of bright red heels, she stood eye to eye with the fireman she was talking to.

I ran up to her and called out to her. "Grandma! Are you okay?" She flashed me a look of disgust before she smiled weakly at the fireman and said something I couldn't make out.

She turned her back to him and grabbed me by the arm. "I told you to never call me that!" She softened her tone then looked me over. "You look exhausted! Was it the flight or riding with that crazy Hattie?" She didn't give me time to answer. "Joe, this is my daughter's daughter, Nikki."

Joe smiled. I wasn't sure if it was his perfectly white teeth that got my attention, his uniform or his sparkling blue eyes, but I was immediately speechless. I tried to say hello, but the words stuck in my throat.

"Nikki, this is Joe Dellucci. He was born in New

Jersey but his parents came from Italy. Isn't that right, Joe?"

I was disappointed when Joe answered without a New Jersey accent. Grandma Dean continued to tell me about Joe's heritage, which reminded me of Hattie. Apparently once you got to a certain age, you automatically became interested in people's backgrounds.

He must have noticed the look of disappointment on my face. "My family moved here when I was ten. My accent only slips in when I'm tired." His face lit up with a smile, causing mine to do the same. "Or when I eat pizza." I had no idea what he meant by that, but it caused me to break out in nervous laughter. Grandma Dean's look of embarrassment finally snapped me out of it.

"Well, Miss Dean. If I hear anything else, I'll let you know. In the meantime, call your insurance company. I'm sure they'll get you in touch with a good fire restoration service. If not, let me know. My brother's in the business."

He handed her a business card and I saw the name in red letters across the front: *Clean-up Guys*. Not a very catchy name. Then suddenly it hit me. A fireman with a brother who does fire restoration? Seemed a little fishy. Joe must have noticed my expression, because he chimed in. "Our house burned down when I was eight and Alex was twelve. I guess it had an impact on us."

Grandma Dean took the card and put it in her back pocket. "Thanks, Joe. I'll give Alex a call this afternoon."

They said their good-byes and as Joe walked away, Grandma Dean turned toward me. "What did I tell you about calling me 'Grandma' in public?" Her voice was barely over a whisper. "I've given you a list of names that are appropriate and I don't understand why you don't use one of them!"

"I'm not calling you Coco!" My mind tried to think of the other names on the list. Peaches? Was that on there? Whatever it was, they all sounded ridiculous.

"There is nothing wrong with Coco!" She pulled away from me and ran a hand through her hair as a woman approached us.

"Geraldine, I'm so sorry to hear about the fire!" The woman hugged Grandma Dean. "Do they know what started it?"

"No, but Joe's on it. He'll figure it out. I'm sure it was wiring or something. You know how these old buildings are."

The woman nodded in agreement. "If you need anything, please let me know." She hugged Grandma again and gave her a look of pity.

"Bev, this is my…daughter's daughter, Nikki."

I rolled my eyes. She couldn't even say granddaughter. I wondered if she would come up with some crazy name to replace that too.

"It's nice to meet you," Bev said without actually looking at me. She looked worried. Her drawn-on eyebrows were pinched together, creating a little bulge between them. "If you hear anything about what started it, please be sure to let me know."

Grandma turned to me as the woman walked away. "She owns the only other antique store on this block. I'm sure she's happy as a clam that her competition is out for a while," Grandma said, almost with a laugh.

I gasped. "Do you think she did it? Do you think she set fire to your shop?"

"Oh, honey, don't go jumping to conclusions like that. She would never hurt a fly." Grandma looked around. "Where's your luggage?"

I turned to point toward Hattie's car, but it was gone.

Grandma let out a loud laugh. "Hattie took off with your luggage? Well, then let's go get it."

2

BY THE TIME we got my luggage and pulled up at Grandma's retirement village, I was exhausted. She took her keys out of her purse and walked toward her apartment, and I walked slowly behind her, lugging my old suitcase. I'd had that old thing for years and yet this was the first time I had ever used it.

Before we entered her apartment, I looked around. The grass was the greenest I had ever seen. A three-tiered fountain that looked like a giant birdbath was the focal point. It had a ledge around it and I imagined it would be the perfect place to sit and read a book. Beautiful flowers in all colors were planted here and there. Buttonwoods, oaks, and a few crepe myrtles dotted the property.

Grandma finally got the key in the door and we walked right into her dining room. I was immediately taken back by how bright the apartment was, and how modern. The entire apartment was bright white with accents in black and red. It looked like something out of a magazine.

Grandma walked into the kitchen, which was to the left of the dining room. "Would you like some water?"

"No, thanks." I put my luggage down and took a look around. It was an open concept home, which I wasn't used to. The farmhouses in Central Illinois where I grew up had many small rooms, all of which were closed off to one another. I liked it that way—lots of places you could run off to and have some time alone to think. Where would you do that here? Your bedroom, I guessed.

The dining room led straight into the living room. The wall furthest from me was nothing but windows and a door that led outside. I walked over to it and peeked out. The apartments in the retirement village created a large rectangle with a pool in the very center. That meant every apartment had a view of the water. The only thing that separated the pool from the apartments was a wide sidewalk.

Grandma walked into the room, swallowing her pills and washing them down with a glass of water. "Come on. I'll show you your room."

I followed her down a small hallway off the dining room. "This is the half-bath." She flicked on a light, revealing a black and white tiled floor, black walls, a pedestal sink and a toilet. I glanced at the art on the wall before she flicked the light off—black and white portraits of her when she was a dancer. I had seen the pictures many times, but they still took my breath away. "Only the guests use this bathroom. You have your own off your room." She pointed to the right. "Your room is this way."

She led me to my room and opened the door. It had the same black and white color scheme as the rest of the house—white walls and carpet with a black and white comforter on the bed. Since the room was at the front of the apartment, I got a view of the fountain and the flowers…and the parking lot. She showed me my bathroom and then opened the door to the walk-in closet. I was shocked.

My first thought was that the closet was big enough to be another bedroom, but then my eyes focused on its contents and I was confused. Hanging from hangers were tiny little clothes.

Grandma Dean read the look on my face. "My cats are giving up their bedroom for you, but I don't have room to keep their clothes elsewhere. I'm afraid you'll have to share a closet with them."

I looked at the outfits that were organized by color —there had to be a hundred of them. There were also boxes labeled "Cat Christmas Decorations" and "Cat Halloween Costumes." The one that intrigued me the most was "Dress Up Outfits," but I figured it was better not to ask.

Grandma Dean took me to the other end of the hall where her bedroom was situated. It was slightly bigger than mine, but the layout of the closet and bathroom was the same.

Once the tour was over, we retreated to the living room. We had eaten dinner after getting my luggage from Hattie, and all I wanted to do was climb in bed and sleep for days. But I didn't think that was polite, so I sat on one of the black leather chairs across from the couch and listened as Grandma called for her cats.

"They like to hide under my bed," she said when they didn't come right away. She called them again. "Hey, my little sweeties! Come give mommy some love!"

Slowly, two cats emerged from the hallway. One jumped up next to her, a fluffy gray cat with large blue eyes, and the other, a white and brown one, lay at her feet. She fluffed the gray one's hair and kissed its face. "This is Kitty Purry." She rubbed behind its ears and it purred loudly. "And that one is Catalie Portman." She bent over and ran her hand down its back.

I laughed inside at the name of her cats. Leave it to Grandma to name her cats after celebrities. She had practically been a celebrity herself at one time, and she had a hard time letting go of that lifestyle.

"I'll be right back." She kissed Kitty Purry on the head and disappeared into the hall. When she came back, she was holding something in her hands. Catalie

Portman took off into the dining room, but Kitty Purry stayed put.

"Time for your jammies!" Kitty Purry jumped on her lap and Grandma slipped a silky pink nightgown over her little fluffy head. She pulled her arms through and patted her on the head. "Would you like a bedtime treat?" She talked to her cat like she was talking to a baby.

Grandma Dean stood to get the cat her treat and I wondered why she didn't bring pajamas for the other one.

Grandma laughed when I asked her. "Oh, Catalie Portman doesn't wear clothes. She's scandalous like that."

With that, she went to the kitchen and I could hear her getting something out of a glass bowl. "Would you like anything?" she hollered at me from the kitchen. "A glass of water? A protein bar? An orange?"

I didn't want anything except to go to bed. I told her good night and made my way to my room. I knew I needed to call my mother and let her know I made it okay. I didn't really want to deal with her questions and I didn't want to tell her about the fire at Grandma's shop and worry her, but I also knew that if I didn't call her, she would call me.

I slipped into my pajamas and noted how much nicer Kitty Purry's were than mine. I brushed my teeth and climbed into bed. I immediately fought to stay awake. My body sunk into the mattress like I was on a cloud. It was the most comfortable bed I had ever been in.

My mom answered on the first ring. "I wondered when you were going to call me." I could hear little kids in the background and knew my sister and her little ones must be visiting. "How was your flight?"

"Long."

Grandma knocked on the door and peeked her head inside. When she saw I was on the phone, she silently apologized. She pointed to the closet and I nodded. She disappeared inside and came out with what I assumed was Kitty's outfit for the next morning. She smiled as she walked out the door, closing it behind her.

"I can't talk long. I'm exhausted after the day I've had."

"How's your grandmother?" My mom completely ignored my not so subtle hint that I didn't want to be on the phone. "Is she well? Staying out of trouble?"

"She's fine. You should see her apartment. It looks like something you would see in a magazine." I let out a laugh and lowered my voice. "And she has pictures of herself in every room."

"And not a single one of her grandkids, I assume." My mother was right. There wasn't a single one of me or my sister Amber anywhere. Also lacking were any pictures of Amber's kids, which I knew my sister had sent in her last Christmas card.

Before I could answer her, I heard a man's voice in

the background. I knew it wasn't my dad so that meant it had to be Amber's husband, Trevor. I couldn't stand him and the feeling was mutual.

"What did he say?" I practically shouted into the phone.

"Oh, just ignore him." My mother didn't want to get involved in our petty arguments, but the fact that she was chuckling at whatever he said irritated me even more. That and I could hear Amber laughing in the background.

"Tell me what he said!"

"Oh, calm down. He was only joking. He just wanted to know if you had married anyone there yet."

"He's just pissed because I married and divorced his older brother...and his younger one."

My mom let out a laugh and now it was my sister who demanded to be told what was said.

"Nikki said Trevor is just pee streamed that she married and divorced two of his brothers."

"Mom! I didn't say 'pee streamed'!"

"I know," she said with a bit of scolding to her voice. "But I'm not going to use your word!"

I could hear my sister and Trevor laughing in the background and didn't know if it was because of what I said or because of some other comment that was made that I didn't hear. Either way, it just made me want to get off the phone even more.

"Mom, I'll call you tomorrow. I really need to get some sleep."

"Okay, honey. Keep an eye on your grandma, will you? Even though that woman irritates me, I still worry about her." I knew the feeling.

I got off the phone and sunk down into the mattress. As tired as I was, Trevor's comment kept me from falling asleep. The fact that I had married and divorced two of his brothers, plus another four men in our little town, was what had me running off to Florida. Well, that and the fact that I was on my way to marriage number seven.

I reached over, grabbed my purse from the nightstand, and pulled out a little coin purse. Zipped safely away was the engagement ring Bo had given me three weeks ago. I slipped it on my finger. It was beautiful, and the first real engagement ring I had ever had. Maybe that was because it was the first real relationship I had ever had.

I sighed at how ridiculous that sounded. My first real relationship and yet I had been married six times? I slipped off the ring and put it back in the coin purse, pulling out a picture of Bo. Man, was he sexy. His blond hair and blue eyes and farmer's tan was everything a girl could dream of.

I hadn't meant to be a serial bride. I married my first husband when I was eighteen. I was young and stupid. I married my second when I was twenty. I was a little older but still stupid. I married my third when I was twenty-three. Older still, but still just as stupid. Now with six under my belt and possibly another one in the future, I could see the only thing changing here was my age.

Thankfully, all of my marriages ended peacefully and without children or property to split, so they were easy and relatively cheap.

My thoughts drifted to my latest fiancé. Out of all my proposals, this was the first that didn't start with, "I'm bored. What do you want to do?" His was an actual down on one knee, stars in the eyes, ring in the box kind of proposal. And it scared me more than it thrilled me. The others had been fun and wild, but this was real.

I also cared about him more than the others. The others were just as stupid as I was. But not Bo. He was loving and caring. He talked about the future and planned for it. He was an adult. I shuddered at the thought. This was a marriage I wouldn't get out of so easily, and it terrified me.

It had been my mother who suggested I go live with Grandma Dean for a little while to get some "clarity." I hated the idea at first, but after a few days, I realized she was right. A little time away would be good for me. I needed to get away from my small farm town—the one where I had married and divorced four percent of the population—and find out what I really wanted in life.

Saying goodbye to Bo had been the hardest thing. I'd never forget the hurt in his eyes, but I thought deep down, he knew it was best. He was understanding about all of the husbands before him, but he had to fear at some level that he would end up just like them. He told me he would wait for me. I looked at his picture and my heart flooded with love for him. He really was the one for me. And not just for three weeks or five months like the others, but for eternity.

3

I HAD NEVER BEEN a fan of coffee, but as soon as the smell of it drifted into my bedroom, I knew I needed a cup. I made my way to the kitchen where Grandma Dean was standing at the counter, flipping through a newspaper.

"Granola?" She extended her arm and handed me a bag that looked like it was full of tiny brown rocks mixed with a few smaller blue ones.

"Do you have donuts?" I handed the bag back to her. There was no way I was going to eat something that looked like it belonged in the bottom of a fish tank.

Grandma Dean scoffed. "What are you? Ten? Healthy adults don't eat donuts for breakfast."

"Who said I was healthy?"

Grandma huffed and filled a bowl with the tiny pebbles and handed it to me. "There's milk in the fridge."

She spoke in the kind of tone that told me there was no getting out of it, so I took the bowl and looked in the refrigerator for the milk. "I don't see any," I said while moving around the few things in the fridge.

"It's right there!" She moved me aside and pulled out a carton that said almond milk. I had never heard of such a thing. I grew up on a farm and worked on one taking care of horses. Milk came from cows, not almonds.

She ignored my dirty looks and poured the milk herself, handing the bowl back to me with a spoon. "Eat it," she commanded.

I sighed and took a bite. I hated to admit it, but it was pretty good. As I finished the last bite, there was a knock on the door. We could see through the window that it was Joe the hunky fireman.

"Quick!" Grandma said, shoving me toward the hallway. "Hide!"

"But why?" I pouted.

"Because you look terrible!"

I wanted to argue, but she was probably right. She looked perfectly put together with her short, straightened hair, her skinny jeans and black tank top. She had a black silky scarf with tiny pink flamingoes scattered on it tied around her neck. Her hot pink heels clicked against the floor as she made her way to the door.

"Hey, Joe!" I heard her say as she opened the door. "What brings you over so early?"

I peeked around the corner into the dining room. He was seriously hot. I was suddenly glad I was hiding.

"Well, Miss Dean, I'm afraid I have some bad news."

Grandma invited him in and he sat at the table while she poured him a cup of coffee and handed him a Danish that had magically appeared out of nowhere. Where were those ten minutes ago?

"What's going on?" she asked him as she sat down in the chair next to his.

"I shouldn't be here telling you this, so you have to promise you won't say anything to anyone."

I heard Grandma promise, a distinct sound of fear evident in her voice.

"That fire at your shop yesterday? It was arson."

He gave Grandma Dean a few minutes to let his words sink in. I was suddenly sick to my stomach. I wanted to rush out there and ask him a million questions, but I stayed in my hiding spot in the hall.

"Are you sure?" Grandma's words were quiet and I could tell she was having a hard time believing the news. "Someone did this to me on purpose?"

"We're sure. The fire was started in the back of your shop near your storage area. I'm so sorry, Geraldine. I really am. Do you have any idea who would do this to you?"

"I have no idea." My heart broke for Grandma Dean. Her voice cracked for a moment and I knew she was holding back tears. She was a strong woman, but this news was more than she could handle.

Grandma was silent for a moment and I heard Joe stand and move his chair back. "I have to go. The chief said he'd come by later today to talk to you. And I'm sure the police will want to talk to you again too. Don't worry, Miss Dean. They'll catch whoever did this."

Joe let himself out and as soon as I heard the door close, I rushed to the table. "Grandma, I'm so sorry." I sat down next to her and put my hand on top of hers. I had never seen her like this before. She was pale and I could feel her hand shaking underneath mine.

She looked up at me and all of a sudden, I saw a fire in her eyes. She stood up quickly. "Put yourself together," she demanded. "We're going down there."

"I'm sorry, Miss Dean. It's a crime scene now. I can't let you in there." Detective Owen Russell was delivering news that Grandma Dean didn't want to hear.

"But this is my shop!" she shouted. "I have every right to go in there!"

"Not right now, you don't. We're doing our best to find out who did this and the crime scene needs to stay clean. As soon as we have what we need, we'll let you in."

"The longer that water stays in there the more damaged things will be!"

"I understand that, Miss Dean. And we're working

as fast as we can. I'll let you know as soon as I can when you can come back. Until then, just go home and rest knowing we have our best men on this."

Grandma Dean sighed and shook her head. She looked up at her shop and fought back her tears. The windows were all broken and had been boarded up, black streaks from the smoke covered the front door and the brick exterior. The large sign that hung on the front of the building sat propped up against the neighboring store.

"Can I take that?" Grandma asked the detective, pointing to the sign.

He looked around as if to see if anyone was watching. "I don't see why not. I'll help you with it."

"No," she told him firmly. "I've got it."

Grandma Dean walked over to the large sign and picked it up. Without turning back to me, she took off toward her car.

"I'm sorry, Detective Russell. She's not handling this very well."

"Please, you can call me Owen. And believe me, she's handling this better than most people. Everyone in town knows your grandmother. She's a well-respected person in this community. I just can't imagine who would do something like this."

"So you have no leads?"

"Not yet, but this is still early in the investigation." He looked around again then lowered his voice as he spoke. "She was clearly targeted. Whoever did this took special precautions to make sure the other shops on either side of her had as little damage as possible."

"How did they do that?"

"I can't say right now. I shouldn't even have said as much as I did." He fidgeted for a moment then looked at me. "I care a lot about your grandmother. I don't have any family here and she's been like family since I moved here two years ago.

There was something about this man that I instantly liked. Maybe it was his dark eyes that seemed to show his kind heart, maybe it was that he was confiding in me moments after we met, or maybe it was how strong he came across and how safe I felt standing right next to him. Whatever it was, I wanted to stand next to him a little longer.

"Do you want to meet for coffee later?" His strong air seemed to weaken a little.

I stumbled for my words, completely taken off guard by his question.

"I just thought maybe I could ask you a few questions, see if maybe there was something your grandmother told you that maybe she's afraid to tell us."

"Oh, sure," I said regaining my composure. "I can do that. But you probably know more about her than I do."

I felt stupid saying that. Shouldn't I have known

more about my own grandmother than this guy? But the truth was that I didn't.

He didn't seem to believe me or if he did, he didn't care. He handed me his business card. "I'm free tomorrow afternoon. There's a coffee shop at the corner." He pointed in the direction of the shop. "Let's meet at three."

I took the card and nodded in agreement. Without another word, he turned and walked away. I made my way to Grandma Dean's car.

"What took you so long?"

She was clearly irritated.

"I was just talking to Detective Owen for a minute."

She looked down and saw his card in my hand. "What's that for?" she asked with her eyes squinted in suspicion.

"We're meeting tomorrow afternoon for coffee," I said, slipping the card into my purse.

Grandma was silent for a moment. "Good thinking!" she said, turning on the car. "You can act like you're interested in him and then find out all he knows! A man like that will spill all his secrets to a beautiful woman!"

For a moment, my head filled with pride. I sat up a little taller and glanced in the side view mirror. I did look pretty good today, didn't I!

I felt Grandma Dean's eyes drilling in to me. She looked me up and down and sighed. "You won't get many secrets looking like that, though. You need a makeover."

Just like her shop, my pride went up in flames and was gone in a flash.

4

"GRANDMA, I don't see why I need to wear all of this!" My protests were completely ignored.

"What do you think, Kitty Purry?" Grandma asked the cat. "Do you think she needs more rouge?"

Kitty tilted her head like she was seriously thinking it over, then she meowed. Apparently, she said yes.

"I can't believe you're going to take that cat's advice!" I said, pushing away the make-up brush.

Grandma paused and thought it over. "You're right. This is more of a question to ask Catalie Portman. Kitty usually does go a little overboard with the makeup."

She hollered twice for Catalie Portman before finally going off to look for her. I took advantage of her absence and quickly wiped off some of the eye shadow and lipstick. It wasn't long before she was back with the cat and I had to hide the makeup-stained tissue.

She sat Catalie on the counter and turned her to look at me. "What do you think? Does she need more of anything?"

Catalie stared at me for at least a full minute. "Oh come on, Grandma, this is ridiculous!" I objected.

"Shhhh," she hissed. "She's thinking!"

I sat there feeling like an idiot for at least another thirty seconds before the cat meowed and jumped off the counter.

Grandma puffed up with pride. "She thinks you look perfect!"

Thirty minutes and one long lecture about my lack of fashion sense later, I was on my way out the door.

"Are you sure you'll be okay?" I felt bad leaving Grandma Dean just a day after she found out someone had purposefully set fire to her antique store.

"I'll be fine." She was practically pushing me out the door. "Go and have fun! And make sure you come back with some information. Oh!" she yelled as I neared the parking lot. "And don't wreck my car!"

I sat down and heard the leather seats beneath me squeak a little. This was nothing like my truck back home. My seats had holes in them and the truck smelled like horses no matter how many times I Febreezed the cab. Mountain Dew bottles littered the floor and gum wrappers (some with chewed gum inside) were piled up everywhere next to the Snickers wrappers.

Grandma Dean's car looked like it had just been

driven off the lot and it smelled like freshly baked cookies…with not a crumb in sight.

I was a nervous wreck as I tried to make my way to the coffee shop. I had taken careful notes on the way home yesterday so I would know how to find it today. I was happy when I took a right and the downtown area appeared up ahead.

"You found it!" Detective Owen Russell stood to greet me when I walked in the door of the coffee shop. His dark hair and dark eyes made him instantly likeable. He was wearing khakis and a red polo shirt with sleeves that hugged his biceps. He looked like he had just stepped out of a J. C. Penney catalog…or one of those catalogs that sold men's underwear. Whatever catalog he stepped out of, I definitely wanted to order it all.

"I know. I'm feeling pretty proud of myself at the moment."

He returned my smile and I joined him at the table.

"I hope you don't mind, but I got here early so I went ahead and ordered."

I eyed his giant cinnamon roll. I had only been living with Grandma Dean for two days, but already I felt like I was starving to death. She had zero tolerance for anything she considered unhealthy. Part of me wanted to play the good little girl with self-control and not order anything, but the real part of me—the part that gets the shakes if I don't get sugar—jumped up and ordered not just one cinnamon roll but two.

The look on his face when I returned to our table with a tray full of food told me he was surprised to see what I ordered. Thankfully, he never actually said anything.

"So, how is your grandmother today?" He caught me mid-bite and he had to wait a few seconds for me to answer.

"She's actually doing really well today!" I took a drink of my coffee and added three little cups of cream. How can people drink this stuff black, I wondered. As I stirred and watched the dark and light liquids swirl together, I thought about Grandma Dean. She really was doing well. She had been in a good mood all morning, like nothing had ever happened.

"You're worrying about something," Owen said over his coffee cup. "I can tell."

I shifted in my chair. "I'm not really worried," I said, cutting off another piece of cinnamon roll. "I was just thinking about how happy she seemed today…" I was going to say more, but when I looked up and saw the look he was giving me, I had a terrible feeling in the pit of my stomach.

"Nikki," he said, putting down his cup and leaning over the table a little. "I'm going to ask you something and I don't want you to be offended."

I hated conversations that started out like that. They almost always led to me being offended.

I leaned back in my chair, bracing myself for whatever it was he was going to say.

"Is your Grandmother okay…financially?"

His question caught me off-guard. "What do you mean?"

Owen cleared his throat and laced his hands in front of him on the table. "Has she had any financial trouble lately? Maybe some bad investments, or a retirement account running out?"

I narrowed my eyes at him. What was he really asking me?

"Look," he said in a sweet voice that made me feel sick. "I've known your Grandmother for two years now and I think the world of her, but sometimes money makes us do things we wouldn't normally do, especially if we're running low…"

I cut him off. "She's doing just fine financially! I'm sure she has more money than you'll see in your entire lifetime!"

"Nikki, look, I didn't mean to upset you. It's my job to ask these kinds of things. I have to look at every angle."

"And what angle are you looking at right now?" I was so angry, I felt like my head was going to explode.

Owen sighed. "Your grandmother is going to get a sizeable amount from the insurance company…"

I stood up, furious. "You think she burned down her own shop to collect the insurance money?"

The look on his face told me everything I needed to know. I grabbed my purse and stormed toward the door. Suddenly, I stopped in my tracks. I took a deep breath. I was angry and I wasn't thinking clearly. I was acting like a fool. With one more deep breath, I turned and walked back to the table. Owen smiled as I made my way back and seemed to relax a little in his seat. I gave him a weak smile, then scooped up my cinnamon rolls and stormed back out. I couldn't believe how dangerously close I had been to leaving them there.

I got lost on the drive home to Grandma Dean's apartment. I was so angry I couldn't think straight. How dare he accuse her of something like that! He had seen how distraught she was yesterday!

I pulled over and tried to hold back my tears. I took a big bite of my cinnamon roll and tried to swallow it past the lump in my throat. I felt like such an idiot. I thought Owen had asked me on a date. Instead, he just wanted to get information he could use to arrest my grandma. What kind of monster does that? My embarrassment and anger over the situation quickly turned to guilt when I realized I had eaten both cinnamon rolls...and stolen the plates they had been sitting on. I would have to return the plates later.

I got out of the car and tried to brush the crumbs off my clothes, then I bent over and tried to carefully brush the crumbs from the seat. Grandma would kill me if she saw the mess I had made.

"Nikki?"

The voice behind me made me jump. I turned to see Fireman Joe walking away from his pickup and walking toward me. "Are you okay?"

"I'm fine," I tried to say through a mouthful of cinnamon roll. I blew little pieces of it everywhere as I spoke and I hoped the sun was in his eyes enough that he didn't see it.

"Are you sure you're okay?" The compassion in his voice made me lose it. I burst into tears, spraying another round of cinnamon roll from my mouth. I had to have put half that thing in my mouth at one time. That was what happened when I got upset. It was like an endless game of Chubby Bunny.

Joe wrapped his arms around me while I sobbed and chewed at the same time. I was relieved when I finally swallowed the last bit of the roll. I closed my eyes and took in his scent before I pulled away from him. Dang, he smelled good.

I wiped the tears from my face, feeling foolish now for crying in front of Joe like that.

"So are you going to tell me what happened?" He leaned down toward me as he said it and tucked a piece of my wild hair behind my ear.

I sniffed and wiped my face again, noticing that my hand came away with frosting on it. My gosh, I was such a mess.

"I had a conversation with Detective Owen Russell," I finally answered. Just saying his name made me angry all over again.

"Is everything okay?" Joe's face wrinkled with concern.

"Yes, except that he thinks my grandma caught her

own shop on fire for the insurance money!" I yelled the words, unable to control myself.

"What?" Joe's face took on the same anger that I felt inside. "He knows Geraldine. We all do! She wouldn't do something like that!"

"That's what I told him!" Did I actually tell him that? I wasn't sure exactly what I told him.

Joe was furious. "I know he's a cop and he's got to look into things, but come on! That's a stretch!"

I just shook my head. I didn't know what to say anymore. Suddenly, I thought of my grandmother. "What am I going to tell her we talked about?" I asked Joe. "She knows we went for coffee. She's going to want to know everything!"

Joe was quiet for a moment. "You met for coffee? Like a date?"

"More like an interrogation!" I really had thought it was a date of some sort, but I would never admit that to him...or anyone.

"I think we should keep this to ourselves." Joe put his arm on my shoulder. "If I know your grandma, and believe me I do, she will not react well to this." He shuddered and I wondered what was flashing through his mind.

I took a deep breath. He was right. Grandma would be furious if she found out she was a suspect. And who knew what she would do—probably something that would only make things worse.

"I'll have a talk with him," Joe said as I climbed back

in the car. "I'll find out if he actually has any evidence…"

"He doesn't!" I yelled. "Because she didn't do it!"

"I know she didn't. But I'll find out why he would even consider her a suspect. I'll call you soon and we can get together so I can tell you what I find out."

I was smart enough this time to know it wasn't a date. I thanked him and closed the car door, then watched him walk away in the rearview mirror. Even in my current state, I still noticed how good his butt looked in those jeans.

5

On the ride back to Grandma Dean's apartment, I had wracked my brain trying to come up with some story of what Owen and I had talked about. By the time I was standing at her door, I still had no idea what to say. I opened the door and expected to be bombarded with questions. Instead, I was met with a group of bewildered old ladies staring at me.

Old wrinkled hands snatched things from the dining room table too fast for my eyes to see what they were. "What are you doing back so soon?" Grandma stood up nervously and walked toward me. "You look terrible," she said when she got closer to me. "What happened to you?"

"Nothing," I replied slowly as I looked past her suspiciously. "What's going on here?"

"We're playing cards." Her answer was too fast and

her tone too high-pitched. Something was clearly going on here.

I looked around her at the table. "Where are the cards then?"

All at once there was a flurry of movement at the table as each woman fished in her purse and pulled out a deck of cards. They smiled like they had me.

"If you're playing cards...then why were they in your purses?" Panic flashed across their faces until one old lady with a purple tint to her hair spoke up. "It's a game cool people play. You wouldn't get it."

That was harsh.

A chorus of laughter rang out and I could tell I clearly wasn't wanted here. Whatever they were up to, they wanted it to be a secret. Well, they could have their little secret. I wanted to go lay down.

I tried to squeeze past Grandma, but she put her hand on my arm gently. "Where are you going?"

"To my room. I have a terrible headache."

Nervous coughs made their way around the table.

"You need some sun," Grandma said to me in an overly sweet voice. "Why don't you go sit by the pool for a little bit?" She smoothed my hair like I was a child, then she made a face. She pulled her hand back and held a little piece of cinnamon roll. Her face went red and she shook her head. To her horror, I took it from her and popped it into my mouth. I thought she was going to kill me right there.

"Here, take this." An old lady in a magenta velour

40

tracksuit stuck her hand in her purse and pulled out a tomato. "You can sit outside by the pool and eat this."

"You might need some salt with that." Another lady dug in her purse and pulled out a tiny crystal saltshaker.

Hattie, the lady who had picked me up from the airport, handed me a wintergreen mint and a Reader's Digest magazine.

One by one, they went around the table, pulling odd things out of their purses and handing them to me—an ink pen that was also a flashlight, a bag of cookies that appeared to be snickerdoodles, and a roll of Tums. The last lady handed me a dollar for a "soda pop" at the vending machine by the pool.

Grandma ushered me to the door in the living room that led out to the pool. She had to get the door for me since my hands were full. "You just relax out there and get some sun. I'll come looking for you in a little bit." She smiled at me as she gave me one last little push. I could hear her locking it as soon as the door closed. What could they be doing in there?

Before I had time to come up with an answer, the door flew open again. Grandma stuck her head out and narrowed her eyes. "And don't ever eat anything out of your hair again. For goodness sakes, Nikki, quit acting like a barbarian!"

She slammed the door and I was left holding old lady provisions. I pressed my ear to the door hoping to hear something that might give me a clue as to what was happening inside. All I heard was muffled laughter.

"Oh! That looks like one of Irene's tomatoes. Are you going to eat that?" I spun around, dropping the flashlight pen and the Reader's Digest. I was thankful it wasn't the crystal saltshaker.

I was suddenly face to face with an old man in a speedo. His silky robe made him look like he just got back from the Playboy mansion while his dyed black hair and mustache screamed 1970s used car salesman.

"I'm Lloyd," he said as he leaned against the apartment. "And who might you be?"

"Nikki," I said as I scrambled to pick up the pen and magazine.

"And what is a delicate flower such as yourself doing out here in the sun?" He gave me a look that sent shivers up my spine. This guy was creepy.

"I'm visiting my grandmother," I said, trying to push past him.

He stepped in front of me.

"Oh! I see the resemblance now! You must be Geraldine Dean's granddaughter. She's quite a looker... and so are you." He winked at me and smiled. I nearly threw up.

I turned around and started to walk in the opposite direction when it hit me. Would he know why Grandma Dean was having a meeting at her house today?

"Hey, uh, Lloyd," I said casually as I turned around.

He was leaning against the building now, stretching his calves. I tried not to roll my eyes.

"My grandmother has several friends over right now. Does she normally have meetings on Thursday afternoons?"

He looked around to make sure no one was watching or listening and carefully made his way toward me, almost tiptoeing. He glanced around one more time before he spoke. "They have a secret group and they get together every week."

"Secret group? What kind of secret group?"

He shushed me like I was talking too loudly. "What kind of secret group?" I repeated again, this time in a whisper.

"If you want to come back to my apartment for some wine, I can tell you," he whispered with a sly smile.

"Forget it," I said loudly and then turned to walk away. What a creep.

"Wait," he said, taking a few steps toward me. "I'll tell you." He looked around again. This man was paranoid. "It's kind of like a neighborhood watch. They call themselves the Glock Grannies. You know..." He paused when he saw the confusion on my face. "...like the gun."

"My grandma has a gun?" I nearly shouted the words and he quickly put his finger to my lips to quiet me down. They smelled like hot dogs. "They all have guns. It's their thing."

Was that what they were scrambling to pick up when I walked in?

"You can't tell anyone about it," he said sternly. "It's a secret."

"Well, if it's a secret then why do you know about it?"

"Because," he said, standing tall and puffing out his chest, "Irene sings like a bird in bed. She spills all her secrets."

"Ewww!" I shouted. TMI!

He laughed behind me as I walked away. "I can't help it if I'm like candy to those ladies!"

I shuddered and tried to get the vision of him and Irene out of my mind.

"Wait!" he shouted one more time. "Seriously, are you going to eat that tomato? Nobody grows tomatoes like Irene."

I looked down at the plump bright red tomato sitting in the crook of my elbow. I shoved some things in my pocket and tossed it to him. He could have the tomato, but I was keeping the snickerdoodles.

6

I USED the back gate to escape Lloyd, and was thankful I still had Grandma Dean's keys in my pocket. I jumped in her car and put my head back on the seat with a sigh. I had left my life in Illinois to get some clarity and instead I jumped right into a made-for-TV crime drama. Or at the very least, a dark episode of *Golden Girls*.

I pulled up in front of Bev's antique shop and looked at the sign on the door. She closed in fifteen minutes. Hopefully I could get a vibe if she was guilty or not in that short amount of time.

There was a black and white striped sign hanging over the door. I laughed when I read it. "Bev's Antiques – Yesterday's stuff at today's prices." I didn't know much about marketing, but something told me that wasn't the best way to sell things.

I opened the door, which set a string of jingling

bells in motion. I was immediately hit by the smell of dust and apple cinnamon candles. I wasn't sure which one triggered my allergies, but before I could completely step inside, I was hit with a vicious sneezing spell. The only person in the shop, a kind looking man with white hair and a gentle smile, made his way to me and handed me a tissue that I gratefully took.

"Thank you," I said to him once I finally got control of my nose. "Crazy allergies."

He nodded knowingly. "This place will do that to ya." He looked around to make sure no one was within earshot. "I liked the other antique store better. It's a shame it burned down."

Before I could ask him what, if anything, he knew about Grandma Dean's store, Bev walked in from the back. I couldn't help but see a wash of concern flash across her face when she saw me. She glanced from me to the man who was now across the store going through a box of buttons.

"Well, hello," she said with a forced smile. "You're Geraldine's daughter, right?"

"Granddaughter," I corrected.

"Oh yes." She let out a little chuckle. "Her daughter's daughter."

Her face seemed to lighten a little until we heard the sound of a hundred buttons hitting the floor, rolling here and there across the wooden planks.

"I'm so sorry about that!" The man bent over to pick them up.

Bev's drawn-on brows shot up into perfect arches that nearly reached her hair line, then quickly dropped back down again. "It's all right, Perry. I'll sweep them up in a minute. That will be faster."

He apologized again and then went back to rummaging through the tiny trinkets in the next box.

Bev sighed. "Anyway, what can I do for you? How's Geraldine? Any word on what happened to her shop?"

"Not yet," I lied. I wasn't about to tell her my grandmother was a suspect not only of arson but also insurance fraud.

"Well, that's a shame. I heard it wasn't an accident." She shook her head as she spoke. "Who would do such a thing?"

Before I could answer, she glanced at the man again, which caused me to do the same. He had stopped fidgeting in the boxes and was clearly listening to our conversation. She gave me a disapproving look. Suddenly, I realized that the dirty looks she had given me when I first came in might not have been directed at me after all, but to him.

Perry quickly turned away from us and became interested in a jar of old thread spools.

Bev turned her attention back to me. "So what can I help you with?"

I stood there for a moment not sure what to say. My plan had been to think all of this through on the way over, but instead my thoughts were on Joe, wondering if he would talk to me again after I had made myself look like a blubbering fool.

"Your shop is really cute," I said, looking around and hoping to buy myself some time.

"Thanks." Bev looked around as well. "It's a work in progress." She looked back at me and waited for me to say something...anything.

"How's business?" I asked as I picked up a basket and pretended to be interested in it.

She was silent and I looked up to see her glaring at me.

"It's fine. Why do you ask?"

This wasn't going like I had planned...if I had planned it out, that is.

I shrugged and tried to play it cool—something I had never in my life actually been able to pull off.

"Just wondering." I smiled and tried to change the subject. "You have so many cute things in here..."

Bev saw right through me. "If you have something to say, then just say it."

I might as well be blunt because honestly, I was going to end up being that way whether I meant to or not. I took a deep breath. "It seems to me that the only person who would gain from Grandma Dean's shop burning down is you."

There. I said it.

She breathed in and her Sharpie eyebrows hung just

above her twitching eyes. "You have a lot of nerve coming into my shop and accusing me of arson!"

Perry turned and looked at us nervously. He slowly put down the small items he had in his hand. "I'll come back for these later," he said as he started to back away.

"That's okay, Perry," Bev said without taking her eyes off me. "Just go ahead and take them. You can pay me for them later."

Perry scooped up his little treasures and stuck them in the pocket of his dusty looking green jacket. "Thanks," he muttered as he practically ran out the door.

"If you want to accuse anyone, maybe you should talk to Perry." Her eyes narrowed even further. "Or better yet, your little fireman friend."

She gave me a little smirk and I wanted to slap it right off her face.

"Joe?" I asked. "Why would he have something to do with this?"

Bev laughed. "Everyone in this town has secrets, Nikki. Everyone."

"Oh yeah? And what's yours?" I narrowed my eyes right back at her.

She pointed past me to the door. "Get out of my shop. And I don't ever want to see you in here again."

I stood there for a few seconds more just to show her I wasn't going to run off just because she said to. But then I felt kind of stupid just standing there staring at her.

I made my way to the car and realized as soon as I sat down inside that I still held the basket I had picked up when I was talking to her. I turned it over in my hands, trying to think of what to do with it. I could take it back in...but would that be weird? Plus, I had just been banned from her store. I could mail it to her, I supposed.

I sighed and leaned back in my seat, trying to think of what to do next, when I looked up and saw Bev glaring at me through the window of her shop. Being the mature person that I was, I waved the basket in the air and stuck my tongue out at her. She headed toward the door and I was afraid she was coming after me so I started the car and threw it into reverse. As I backed out of the parking space, I nearly ran over Perry, who was standing too close to the car. It suddenly dawned on me how close he really had been. Was he looking in the car windows when I came out? There wasn't time to figure it out. Right then, I needed to get away from Bev.

When I got back to Grandma's retirement community, I snuck back in through the gate by the pool. I was thankful that Lloyd was nowhere in sight. I sat down in a lounge chair and stared up at the sky. Streaks of pink and purple swept overhead. If I was home in Illinois, I could sit on my front porch and watch the sunset and see not just a small area right above me, but the whole entire sky. My heart ached for all of it—my little house...my family...Bo...

"So, I heard you did a little antique shopping today." Grandma's voice brought me back to reality and I bolted upright in the lounger. "Or should I say some antique stealing?"

Busted.

"Word travels fast in this town," I said, leaning back again, preferring not to look her in the eyes at the moment.

"Yes, it does." She sighed and sat down next to me. "Nikki, what were you thinking? How could you accuse Bev of setting my shop on fire? And stealing?" She sighed again and shook her head. "And I'm not even going to talk to you about how childish you were sticking your tongue out at her."

Wow, Bev didn't leave out a single detail then.

I sat upright again. "Grandma, don't you think she did it? She had a motive even! If she put you out of business, then she would get your customers!"

Grandma Dean leaned forward. "Nikki, I'm the reason she's *in* business. Without me, she wouldn't even have an antique shop."

"What do you mean?" Now I was completely confused.

"This is just between us, okay?"

I nodded in agreement.

"I go to estate sales all over Florida. I go to little markets every chance I get. Heck, I even buy things online. And a lot of what I buy is in bulk. I might buy several boxes of stuff, but I only keep the really nice things, the high end antiques." She paused. "And then I give Bev the rest."

"You mean you sell it to her?"

Grandma was silent for a minute. "No, I give it to her."

"Why would you do that? You could probably double your profits if you made her pay for them!"

Grandma laughed. "That stuff isn't worth that much!" Her face turned serious all of a sudden. "There are things about people you don't know, Nikki. I've lived in this town for a while now. I know people's stories."

"You mean their secrets." It was more of a statement than a question. I wondered if she knew Joe's...or if Bev was just trying to get in my head.

"Bev's story isn't a secret. The only thing that's a secret is that I keep her shop fully stocked. And you promised me you'll keep it that way."

"Yes, but I still don't get why you would do that for her."

Grandma looked up at the sky and for a moment, I thought she was going to change the subject. She turned her attention back to me. "Bev's mother has Alzheimer's. She was diagnosed about five years ago. Bev didn't want to put her in a home, so she let her come live with her and her husband." Grandma shook her head slowly and I could see the compassion flood her face. "Unfortunately, her marriage was already on shaky ground and the stress of Bev's mother was just too much. He left her after six months."

"What a jerk," I said, suddenly feeling sorry for Bev.

"Taking care of someone who is ill is hard on even the strongest marriage. Plus, Bev was a constant nag. I think he might have just been looking for a way out. But whatever the reason, he left and she was alone with mounting bills and here I was with a storage building full of stuff I didn't want to put in my own shop... You can see how we worked things out."

Grandma Dean was a lot of things—fashionable, fun, energetic—but I had never thought of her as someone who could be that kind. I guessed that was her little secret.

"That was really nice of you."

She shrugged it off. "We have to help each other when we can."

I sat there for a moment letting all of this information sink in. There was no way Bev would've burned down Grandma's shop then. Grandma was her lifeline. I had taken her interest in the fire as a sign of guilt, but clearly I was wrong. She was probably just worried about what would happen to her and the constant flow of Grandma's cast-off antiques.

I put my head in my hands and rubbed my temples, trying to keep the shame and guilt at bay. I would have to go back and apologize to her...and bring back her basket. Heck, I might as well do it on the way to return the plates I'd stolen from the coffee shop earlier. It had not been a good day for me.

Suddenly, I remembered Perry.

I looked back at Grandma, who was again admiring the sky. "I met a man today," I started. "His name was Perry. Bev said if I was going to accuse anyone, it should be him." I decided to leave out the part where she also said I should accuse Joe.

"Perry Landon?" Grandma asked. "Late sixties, white hair, kind of shy?"

"Yep, that's the one."

Grandma let out a little laugh. "He's harmless. He comes in my shop all the time... Well, he used to anyway. He was always buying little things." She leaned forward again with a smile. "Here's another little secret for you. I kept a few boxes of tiny little things—broken pieces of jewelry, buttons, worthless coins, things like that—just for him. I don't know why he likes to rummage through that stuff, but he does." She sighed. "I miss my shop. Perry was a little strange and never talked much, but other people did. I knew everything about everyone in this town. Now the only way I find out about anything is when someone calls me." She gave me a disapproving look.

"I'm sorry about that," I apologized. "It won't happen again."

"Ugh, I'd like to believe that," she said, standing up. "But you and I both know that isn't true." She smiled down at me. "Come on, let's go get some dinner. I'm starving."

THAT NIGHT I sat in bed, my mind running through the events of the day. It had been a doozy, as my mother would say. My bedroom door opened a few inches and in walked Catalie Portman. I patted the bed and she jumped up, making herself comfortable next to me.

"Oh, Catalie," I said, stroking her little furry head. "My life is such a mess." She looked up at me as if to say that she understood. I liked Catalie. Kitty Purry was too good for me, but Catalie didn't judge.

I pulled out the picture of Bo. His blond hair was unruly and partially in his blue eyes. His smile was as bright as the sun. He was laughing in the picture. I tried to remember why, but I couldn't. He laughed easily, so it could've been the smallest thing that made him laugh at that moment.

I thought back to a few days ago when I left him. He didn't try to stop me. He was silent, his easy smile hidden away under what I assumed was sadness. Bo had told me that he understood when I said I needed to get away for a little while. I had hoped that he would tell me not to go. Instead, he held me tight that night and when my alarm went off, he let me go. He said good-bye to me at the door and that was it. I didn't know whether to be thankful he was handling it so well or hurt that he didn't try to stop me.

I reached under my pillow and pulled out one of his shirts that I had snuck into my bag. I put it up to my face and breathed in the scent. My heart sank. The familiar scent of his cologne was nearly masked by the scent of Grandma's fabric softener that must have rubbed off from the pillow.

I missed Bo so much. And at the same time I couldn't stop thinking about Fireman Joe. What was wrong with me? Why did I have to mess everything up so much? I could be in Illinois right now planning my wedding...my seventh one. Those last words brought tears to my eyes. I felt like such a failure. If I was honest with myself though, I didn't want any of those other marriages to work out. I had just been working my way through the male members of my high school FFA. Bo was the last one. Who else would there be after him? Was I afraid of marrying him because I knew he was the one? Or because I had finally reached the end of the eligible bachelors in my county?

"Why am I like this, Catalie?" I asked as I ran my hand down her back. But deep down, I knew why.

Bev's words floated through my mind. "Everyone has secrets. Everyone."

I had never told anyone my secret, and as I sat there petting Catalie, pushing back the painful memories, I promised myself I never would.

7

KITTY PURRY WAS DRESSED in a rainbow tutu and a black t-shirt that said "Thug Life." She strutted through the kitchen and I swore Catalie Portman rolled her eyes. I took a sip of my coffee and a bite of my gluten-free toast. I didn't know which one I detested more. I needed an excuse to get out and get some real breakfast.

Thankfully, my cell rang. It was Joe.

"Hey! It's Joe." His voice sounded a little raspy. I assumed he had just woken up. "I have some news about your grandma. Can you meet me today?"

"How about right now!" I looked at my watch. It was eight am, still early enough to get the good donuts at a donut shop, as long as I hurried.

"Right now?" He hesitated and I felt a little guilty suggesting we meet immediately. Did that make me look desperate for something?

"Now works," he finally said. "But...can we meet at my house? I have some information about the case and, don't take this the wrong way, but I don't want anyone to see us talking. I don't want it to get out that I shared anything with you."

So, I thought, *I get to see Joe at his house and get donuts. Sounded like a win-win to me.*

Grandma was out with her cycling team, Life Behind Bars, so I took the extra set of car keys off the hook by the door and left her a note. With any luck, I'd be back before she got home.

Thirty minutes later, I pulled up in front of a two-story brick house surrounded by a metal fence. It reminded me of the fence that was around our playground at my elementary school. A couple dog toys littered the otherwise nicely manicured lawn.

With a dozen donuts in hand, I knocked on the door. Joe answered and he looked exhausted.

"You okay?" I asked as I stepped in.

"Just got off my shift," he said, running a hand through his nearly black hair. "I'm wiped out."

Now I really felt guilty.

"Why didn't you say something on the phone? We could've met this afternoon!"

He led the way to the kitchen and pulled out a chair for me before grabbing a couple of plates for the donuts. "You wanted to meet right away. And I can't blame you. If someone had info on my family, I'd be impatient too."

Oh yes, that was why I wanted to see him, the "info."

He grabbed a chocolate cream-filled out of the box. I expected him to be more of a jelly donut kind of guy.

"You having one?" he asked as he took a bite.

"I'm not really all that hungry." I left out that it was because I had eaten three donuts in the car on the way there.

He finished his donut in four bites and grabbed another one. "I can't tell you where I heard this from, but I know why your grandma is a suspect."

I suddenly felt sick to my stomach. Was it my nerves? The donuts? Whatever it was, I didn't like it.

"They found some papers when they were cleaning up after the fire."

"What kind of papers?" I asked, almost afraid of his answer.

"Late notices. Bills that are overdue. It looks like she owes the city a lot of money. The bills were near the fire. It was almost like she was trying to burn them too."

Anger rose through my body. "She didn't burn anything!" I yelled.

Joe jumped up from the table just as I did. "I didn't mean anything by that, Nikki. I think she's innocent just like you do." He walked over to me and put his hand on my shoulder. "I'm just telling you what I know. I don't believe that she did it. She's too smart for that. Besides, isn't she loaded?"

I sat back down and grabbed a donut from the box. "I think she is, but I'm not sure."

Joe grabbed his chair and brought it closer to my mine. Our knees were touching under the table. "She used to be some kind of celebrity, didn't she?"

"Yeah, not so much here in the U.S. but she did a lot of things in Europe—acting, dancing, and some commercials." I picked at the sprinkles on my donut. "I don't know how much of that money she has left, though." I sighed and pushed the donut away. "I have to go." I got up.

"I'm sorry if I upset you, Nikki," Joe said, standing up with me. "I know this has to be hard on you...and Geraldine."

I looked into his dark brown eyes. He was clearly exhausted and yet he had taken the time to talk to me this morning. "Thank you for letting me come over so early."

"You can come by anytime you want...especially if you bring donuts." He smiled and it made my heart do a little leap.

I looked up at him, not quite ready to go, and yet I felt like I needed to be alone to think for a minute. He reached over and gently grabbed my arm. "If you need to talk, I'm here."

He was just inches away from me and I could feel his breath on my skin. He looked into my eyes and I felt like a magnetic force was slowly pulling us together. My heart pounded in my chest and I was sure it was loud enough for him to hear in the perfectly silent kitchen.

A commotion at the door made us both jump. I spun around to see a man with the same nose and eyes as Joe. I knew immediately it had to be his brother. Even though they looked a lot alike, his brother had more of a boyish look to him. He had hold of a dog leash with a very large dog on one end. The dog plopped down, panting.

"This is my brother, Alex. Alex, this is Nikki."

"Hey, Nikki!" he said, his smile big enough that I could see every tooth.

"Joe, I need you to watch the dog for a sec. Hottie Neighbor is outside and I want to say hi!"

"Why can't you take the dog?" Joe asked.

"Because he smells bad!" He looked down at the dog. "And he's kinda ugly."

Alex dropped the leash and ran outside. Joe turned to get the poor dog a dish of water.

"I don't think he's ugly," I said, bending down to get a better look at him. Then again, maybe he was. And Alex was right. The dog smelled terrible. I looked up at Joe. "What's his name?"

He stammered for a minute then blurted out, "Spot."

I looked back at the dog. He didn't look like a Spot. He was a solid dark gray—not a single spot in sight.

"Come here, Spot," I said, taking the dish from Joe and putting it in front of me. "Do you want a drink?"

Spot looked at me but didn't move. "Spot, come here," I said again, this time patting my legs and inviting him to come closer to me. He didn't budge.

"He's not very friendly," Joe said, giving me a hand up.

I looked back at the dog. He seemed friendly when Alex brought him in. I always thought of myself as a dog person. Dogs always liked me. Maybe he was getting a weird vibe from me since I spent all day around cats now.

I turned back around and saw that Joe was standing right behind me with the box of donuts. "Thanks for coming by," he said as he herded me toward the door. His sudden change in demeanor caught me by surprise. I felt like he was trying to get rid of me. Maybe it was that neighbor. Maybe Joe had a thing for her too. I sighed and waved off the donuts. I certainly didn't need anymore. "No," I said, standing in the middle of his living room. "You can keep them."

Just then Alex burst through the door again. That guy did not know how to make a quiet entry.

"Dude! I think I'm wearing her down! I asked her to go bowling with me and she said she didn't like bowling!"

Joe and I looked at each other, not understanding the excitement in his voice when clearly this was not good news for him.

Alex looked at us like we were idiots. "Hello!" he yelled. "She didn't come right out and say no this time!"

"Ohhh," we said in unison.

"Well, that's great!" Joe said, clapping him on the back. "It won't be long now and the two of you will be sending out the wedding invites."

Alex smiled proudly and puffed out his chest. "You'll be my best man, right?" he asked Joe.

"Of course I will, buddy."

The brothers were so cute together. There was something very simple and childlike about Alex. His excitement for life was contagious. I could tell he was the kind of guy that made everyone laugh and feel welcome. I liked him immediately. Then again, I liked most guys immediately—hence the six ex-husbands.

Alex looked past us. "You didn't take the leash off the dog?"

"I tried to get Spot to come to me so I could take it off, but he wouldn't." I couldn't help but see Joe cringe when I spoke.

Alex laughed. "Spot? Well, that's the problem. He only answers to his name."

I shot a confused look to Joe, who tried to quickly push me to the door. I stood firm in my place and looked around him. "What's his name then?" I asked Alex.

Alex bent down and called the dog. "Come here, Arson, let's get that leash off of you."

I looked at Joe. "Arson? Seriously? Your dog's name is Arson?"

Joe started to say something, but Alex interrupted.

"Yep, that's his name. Arson, the ugliest, smelliest dog on the block." He looked at me with his childlike smile. "Of course that's his formal name. We just call him Arson for short."

"Well, like I said," Joe said, trying again to push me to the door. "I'm glad you stopped by."

I gave him a look that let him know he seriously better stop pushing me. He sighed and stepped aside in a show of surrender.

"Alex, why is your dog named Arson?" I asked suspiciously. I knew better than to direct the question to Joe. I was sure he wouldn't give me a straight answer. Alex, on the other hand—I didn't think he would lie about anything.

"Oh, he's not our dog. He's our cousin Eddie's. We're just watching him until he gets out of prison."

My eyebrows shot up and I looked at Joe. "Why is he in prison?"

"He may have set a house or two on fire." Joe spoke so quietly I could barely hear him.

Alex's laughter filled the room. "May have? Ha! He was a volunteer for his local fire department. On days when things were slow, he'd go out and start fires just so him and his fire buddies would have something to do!"

I gasped. "That's horrible. Were the other guys in on it too?"

"Nah," Alex said, scratching Arson behind the ears. "They had no idea...at first. After a few months, they

64

started to get suspicious. Eventually, they caught him."

"How many things did he set on fire?" I was almost afraid of the answer.

"Fifteen, but only two were houses—both ex-girlfriends. He mostly set fire to barns and out buildings."

"Why did you lie to me?" I quietly asked Joe.

"I saw the look you gave me on the day we first met when I told you I was a fireman and my brother owned a fire restoration business. You obviously thought that was weird. I wasn't going to tell you I had a cousin in prison for arson. I didn't want you to think we all worked together."

I scoffed at him. "I wouldn't have thought that." I totally would've thought that.

Joe shrugged. "I would just hate for word to get out. He lived a few hours away and I hope the stories stay over there. I don't want people in this town feeling like they can't trust me."

This must have been the secret Bev was talking about. Obviously, the stories of Cousin Eddie had crossed the county line. I didn't have the heart to tell Joe.

I looked back at the dog, who was now chewing on a giant dog toy. "Why would he name his dog Arson?" I asked, almost to myself.

"We think it was a cry for help," Alex said, standing up. "I'm going to take the other dog for a walk now. I don't like walking them together. I get all tangled up in their leashes. Last week, I walked them together and everything was going fine until we got in front of Hottie Neighbor's house." He shook his head and let out a laugh. "Dumb dogs got all excited and somehow I got all wrapped in their leashes. They took off running and drug me about three blocks." He pulled up his sleeve showing a big patch of flesh. "It took my skin right off." He laughed again. "Crazy dogs."

He cupped his hands to his mouth and called out. "Blaze! Wanna go for a walk?"

A yellow lab came bounding down the stairs, wagging his tale and doing circles around Alex.

I rolled my eyes at Joe. "Blaze?"

He shrugged his shoulders and repeated what his brother had just said. "Cry for help."

Joe walked me outside and we stood on his little front porch. I could see Hottie Neighbor next door in her super short shorts, bent over watering her dead flowers. She turned her head and smiled at Joe, giving him a little wink.

Joe let out a little giggle and I gave him a dirty look. "You disgust me."

"What did I do?" he asked. "I'm just being friendly."

I started to walk down the steps and he grabbed my arm. "If I cared about Hottie Neighbor..." He stopped and corrected himself. "...my neighbor, would I do this?"

He pulled me close and kissed me. At first, I

couldn't hear anything over the angels singing Hallelujah in my ear. But then I heard Hottie Neighbor's door slam shut.

When he gently pulled away, I was speechless.

"I'm sorry," he said, shaking his head. "I don't know what got into me."

Part of me wanted to grab him and knock him to the floor and really make Hottie Neighbor jealous, but part of me took a step back and looked at the whole situation. I was supposed to be in Florida to learn about myself, to stop making the same mistakes over and over again. I didn't mean that Joe would be a mistake, but it wasn't the right time to start something with him—no matter how tempting it was.

"I just… I can't do this right now." I saw the look of disappointment on his face when I said it.

"I understand. I'm so sorry," he apologized again.

I knew he didn't actually understand. He didn't know why I was there—why I had left everything and moved in with my grandma. For a brief moment, I thought about telling him, but no matter how much of a positive spin you try to put on being married six times and having a fiancé back home, you still come out looking like a lunatic. I would rather leave with him feeling embarrassed about my knowledge of cousin Eddie then my feeling embarrassed because he knew about my husbands…ex-husbands.

I gave him a smile and punched him in the arm. "Let me know if you hear anything else about my grandma."

He nodded and I turned away, walking down the few steps to the sidewalk. I heard him go inside and close the door, but at the same time I felt like someone was watching me. I turned to see Hottie Neighbor looking at me through a window. I smiled and waved wildly. She gave me a dirty look and pulled her curtains together with enough force that the curtain rod fell down.

It wasn't every day that I made someone that looked like that jealous. I couldn't help but puff up with a bit of pride. Donuts, a kiss from Joe, and I ticked off Hottie Neighbor—all before 10am. This was going to be a very good day.

I climbed in Grandma's car and suddenly remembered the news that Joe had given me. Grandma Dean looked guilty because she owed the city a ton of money. My heart sank. Could she really be guilty? Would she really have set her shop on fire to collect the insurance money to pay off her debt? I was going to have to figure out a way to talk to her about her finances and find out for myself if she was in financial trouble. Man, this day was going to suck.

8

When I walked through the door, I called out to Grandma but she didn't answer. I hung the spare key on the hook and checked each room to make sure she wasn't there. I was glad she wasn't home yet. That gave me time to snoop around a little.

I looked through the kitchen drawers and was surprised by what I saw. Several of the drawers were empty and the ones that did have something in them were neatly organized in little trays.

I moved into the living room and rolled up the door on the small secretary desk. One drawer had a book of stamps, another had two black pens. I turned around and thought for a minute. I was tempted to take a peek in her room, but that felt wrong. Instead, I scanned the living room trying to think of someplace else to look.

Two end tables flanked the couch and another small table sat between the two chairs in front of the large picture window. I opened the drawer on the small table first. Inside was a little black notebook. I nervously picked it up and turned to the first page. There was a name of a veterinarian from the All Animals Pet Clinic and a phone number. I turned to the next page and heaved a little. It was Kitty Purry's poop schedule on August 19th, 2015. I turned the next page and it was more of the same. Yuck. I threw the notebook back in the drawer and closed it with a shudder.

I walked across the living room and knelt down to open the end table door. Inside were stacks of photo albums. I took out the first one and was amazed by what I saw. The first page was a black and white headshot of Grandma Dean. She was beautiful with her shoulder-length hair curled slightly and her creamy looking skin. Her teeth were perfect and her lips were plump. Even though all that had changed over the years, one thing stayed the same—she still had that same sparkle in her eyes.

I smiled as I flipped the page, revealing other headshots and some full-length photos. She was absolutely stunning.

I was so caught up in the pictures that I didn't hear Grandma Dean come in.

"What are you doing going through my things?"

I jumped, throwing the photo album back into the end table.

Grandma laughed. "I'm just kidding. You can look

at those." She sat on the couch. "Grab those and hand them to me."

I reached in and grabbed the stack of albums. I handed her the first one and sat the rest on the coffee table before taking a seat next to her.

"These," she said as she pointed to the headshots, "were taken by Marvin Crenshaw. Anyone who was anyone wanted him to take their picture."

She smiled with pride as she turned the page. She pointed to a picture of her standing next to a piano in a swanky looking club. "This was the first time I ever sang in front of people." She let out a little laugh, shaking her head slightly. "I went to Europe to be an actress but my agent said I should try singing. He booked me at this club to sing during the dinner hour." She laughed again. "I had never sung in my life, not even in the shower! But I put on my prettiest dress and my agent paid someone to do my hair and makeup and I went up there on that stage and I sang my heart out!"

"How did you do?" I asked, hanging on every word.

"I did pretty well! And the more the crowd drank the better I sounded!" We both burst into laughter.

"Did you sing much after that?"

"Oh yes. I was booked every Saturday night. That was a turning point for my career. Before long, I was doing commercials for cigarettes and perfume. Then I went on to do a few movies. That, of course, was my favorite." She paused and I could tell she was picturing the glamor of it all as she smiled to herself. "Being a celebrity was so different back then. It was all about glamor and sophistication. People were real classy. Today, it's all about the attention, and celebrities will do just about anything to get it." She shook her head in disgust. "It's a real shame."

Grandma put the photo album on the floor and picked up another one from the coffee table.

"Oh, this one is fun! This is when I did that soap opera. I barely spoke a word of French in the beginning and my accent was awful. But I had the right look, so they cast me as Sophia—the innocent girl next door who wasn't so innocent."

She flipped through page after page of her and the cast being glamorous on set, then being glamorous off set. She looked perfect in every one. When I pointed that out, she laughed. "That," she said with a chuckle, "is what happens when people have hair and makeup artists to make them up each day. See this guy right here?" She pointed to a man with sleeked back black hair and a perfect jaw line. "Isn't he attractive?"

I nodded.

"You take off all the makeup and he's seriously the ugliest man you've ever seen! Red blotchy face, an eye that sags a little... How they made him look like that, I'll never know. It must be some kind of voodoo."

Grandma sat the album aside and grabbed a third one. Her bright smile softened and she grew quiet. "This one is when Glenn and I went to Paris."

She opened the album and ran her finger along the

face of a man that I instantly recognized. Grandpa Glenn. She sighed and sat there, quietly staring at him.

I remembered very little about Grandpa Glenn. When he and Grandma Dean came to visit, it was always a whirlwind. They would come in the afternoon, bringing expensive gifts that my sister and I didn't know what to do with, then Grandma and Glenn would be gone by the time we went to bed that night.

Grandma was always loud and laughed as she told stories. She always seemed like someone straight out of a movie—maybe because sometimes she was. I sat there trying to think of some of the stories she told, but I couldn't think of anything. The only thing I remembered about them was my mother, gasping in horror and trying to cover our ears while shouting, "Mother, not in front of the kids!" She would then tell us it was bedtime and order us to our rooms. We'd pass Grandpa Glenn on the way out of the living room. He was always quiet and hung back, smoking his cigar. As we walked by him, he'd stick his hand out and give us a half-dollar. He'd wink and we'd smile back before heading upstairs to our rooms.

"I wish I remembered more about him," I said, breaking the silence.

"He was a wonderful man. I fell in love with him the moment I saw him. I was in New York at a party. I was nineteen and he was thirty. He told me he was an agent and he had an opportunity for me if I was interested in going to Europe. Well, I jumped at the chance! My career was going nowhere fast in the States. There was only one problem…"

She stopped and closed the book, letting it rest on her lap. Her face fell and I waited to see if she was going to continue. She put the album aside and looked at the cover of the three albums left on the coffee table. She selected one and opened it. The first picture was a birth announcement from a local newspaper. The second page was a very young Grandma Dean holding a baby. She sighed heavily. "That's your mother." Her face warmed and she smiled gently. "She was a beautiful baby, perfect in every way."

She turned the pages and I saw my mother sleeping on the floor next to a little dog and another photo of her in the bathtub. My favorite was her in nothing but a cloth diaper and a bonnet, cradling a baby doll. "She was probably a year and a half," Grandma Dean said, admiring the picture.

I held my breath as she pointed out a picture here and there, telling me a little story about each one as she flipped through the pages. She had never talked to me about my mother's father before. All I knew was that it wasn't Glenn. And I knew my mother didn't know either. Would she finally share the secrets she'd held close to her heart all those years? I had so many questions, but I didn't want to ask and make her close up. I sat there quietly, listening as little by little she let the pictures take her on a tour of her past.

As we neared the end of the album, my heart sank a

little. She hadn't said anything about my real grandfather. And then she turned to the last page. The photo wasn't tucked safely behind plastic film like the others were. Instead, it was loose and it fell onto Grandma's lap. She picked it up and studied it. A young man with dark hair and glasses dressed in a pair of dress pants and a button-up shirt stood next to a very young Geraldine Baker, Grandma's maiden name. Young Geraldine didn't have the thick makeup and curled hair that she did later when she began her acting career. Instead, her hair was straight and her face looked fresh and makeup free. They looked happy. No, that was an understatement. They looked like they were the happiest people in the world.

"Who is that?" I asked cautiously.

Grandma sighed. "Someone I loved very much." She didn't take her eyes off the photo. "It feels like a lifetime ago, or maybe someone else's life even."

I stared at the man. He looked so much like my mother. They had the same nose, same chin, same sideways smile. I knew Grandma wouldn't tell me the truth of his identity, but she didn't have to. I knew it was my mother's real father.

Grandma took in a deep breath and tucked the picture back into the photo album. She stacked them back up on the coffee table before picking them all up and putting them back in the end table.

"Well," she said, standing up. "That was a long walk down memory lane!" She smiled, but I could tell it was forced. "I'm exhausted after our cycling meeting today. I'm going to take a shower and then take a quick nap. Let's go out for dinner tonight—somewhere fancy!"

She didn't wait for my answer. Instead, she turned and walked into her room. Kitty Purry and Catalie Portman followed her, as if they sensed that she needed them in that moment to quietly comfort her.

I stayed in my position on the couch until Grandma's door was shut, and I gave her plenty of time to get in the shower. Once I felt like it was safe, I rummaged through the end table until I found the photo album I wanted. I flipped to the back and studied the picture for a moment until I flipped it over. Scrawled on the back was 'Thomas and Geraldine 1959.' "His name is Thomas," I whispered to myself. I put the picture back in the album and put it back in its place in the end table.

What Grandma didn't say, but I already knew, was that my mother was eighteen months old when Grandma went to Europe. Her parents were very supportive of her acting and modeling career and they said she could leave my mom, Marilyn, with them. That was what she did. She left her baby and went to follow her dreams, marrying Glenn, her agent, a year later. My mom said she'd forgiven her, but I knew deep down she still held onto the pain of not having her mother when she was growing up. Geraldine would make visits here and there, and send little packages in the mail, but that was no way to build a strong relationship with a child. It wasn't until Grandma came back to the US that they were reunited and began to work on a mother/daughter relationship. But it was always strained, and I thought it always would be.

I stood up, feeling a little depressed. Grandma Dean's past was so full of fun and adventure, but it was also full of pain. Pain is such an interesting thing. It can lie dormant for years, then come back and be as ferocious as the day it came into your life.

Grandma had her secrets. I had mine. Joe had his and Bev had hers. Everyone has secrets. Everyone.

9

When Grandma emerged from her bedroom hours later, she looked like her usual, energetic self.

"I made reservations at The Cobbler's Tea Room."

I tried to hide my disappointment. I was more of a steak and potatoes kind of girl.

Apparently, I didn't hide my disappointment as well as I thought. "Believe me," Grandma assured me, "you'll love it."

She stared me up and down for a minute and I braced myself for the unwanted beauty advice and forced makeover.

"I have a dress that I think might fit you. I'll be right back."

I really didn't want to wear a dress, but I didn't want to upset Grandma Dean, especially after the morning we'd had.

She scooped up Kitty Purry. "You can come help me pick something out," she said to the cat.

As they disappeared into her room, I stood in the half-bathroom off the hall and looked myself over. I liked my hair and makeup-free face just the way they were.

I could hear Grandma Dean coming down the hall and I took a deep breath. Any second she was going to pop her head in the bathroom and hand me a dress, probably something floral or paisley.

To my surprise, she held a simple, black dress in her hand. "Here," she said, handing it to me. "Try it on."

When I closed the door, I took a look at it. It looked small, yet elegant. I got undressed and slipped the dress over my head. I pulled it on and glanced down to see how it looked. It fit like a glove.

The dress was just above the knee and hugged my figure perfectly. Nothing bulged out or hung over. It was like it was made for me.

I looked at myself in the mirror and suddenly I could understand why Grandma cared so much about how she looked. It wasn't to impress people—well, maybe sometimes it was—but it was more because it made her feel good about herself. Suddenly, I wanted perfect hair and makeup to go along with the perfect dress.

I opened the door and Grandma Dean gasped. I spun around a little so she could see the whole thing. "What do you think?"

"It's perfect!" she said with her hands clasped over her mouth. "You look stunning! And I didn't even know you had curves!"

It was a total surprise to me too.

"Let me grab my purse and then we'll go." She started to take off down the hall.

I stood there dumbfounded. What about my hair? My makeup?

"Grandma Dean," I called after her. "What about the make-over?"

"Well," she said, walking back toward me. "I felt a little guilty after Kitty Purry and I did that to you the other day. I know that's not your thing. If you're happy with the way you look then I should be too."

She started back down the hall again to her room.

"But...what if I wanted you to do that? Just for today! You know, because I'm wearing a dress and everything."

I had never seen Grandma Dean move that fast. She was back to the bathroom door in a flash, grabbing my arm and dragging me to her bathroom, all the while talking about color pallets and blending.

She pointed to her vanity. "Have a seat." She looked at her watch. "Hmm, we only have about twenty minutes." She looked me up and down. "We don't have much time so the eyebrows are out. We'll just have to do some gel in the hair to tame that a bit...whew!" She shook her head and grabbed her makeup brushes with determination. "We can do this!"

Twenty minutes later, I looked in the mirror and could barely believe my eyes. My hair was curly but not frizzy, and my makeup wasn't overdone. I had soft pink eye shadow and soft pink lips. A little bronzer across my cheeks, but not too much. A thin layer of eyeliner and a little mascara. I could live with this look!

She gave me a little spritz of her perfume and we were out the door.

When we arrived at the tea room, I was starving. *I'll just have to sneak out later and grab some real food*, I told myself. But when we walked in the door, I was pleasantly surprised.

The restaurant was beautiful. Tables with delicate looking white table clothes were scattered across the large room. Black chairs with white bows surrounded them. Several large black chandeliers gave the room a romantic feel. The place smelled like a mixture of sweet bread and roses.

As we walked to our table, I couldn't help but glance at what others had ordered—tiny sandwiches with different kinds of bread on plates rimmed with gold, scones and other pastries on smaller plates with a tiny floral trim. Glasses half-full of wine, tea, and sparkling drinks with a wedge of fruit perched on the side. It almost looked too beautiful to be real.

I looked up and saw a man playing the violin in the corner. The sound drifted through the air and mingled with the hushed voices of the customers. Clinking glasses and gentle laughter said that this was a happy place to be.

On our way to our table, Grandma Dean saw someone she recognized. We stopped for a moment so she could say hello to the woman in her mid-fifties who was seated next to someone closer to Grandma's age.

"Mitzie McCreedy, how are you, dear?"

"I'm doing well...under the circumstances." The woman stood and hugged Grandma Dean, then sat down again.

"When you came in my shop last week and told me about your mother, I was just heartbroken. How much longer will be you in town?"

"Just a few more weeks. Just trying to tie up loose ends."

As the two talked, I couldn't help but notice the older lady sitting at the table scowling at Grandma. Then I realized that Grandma had never greeted her. I thought that was interesting. Grandma Dean talked to everybody.

"Well, it was good to see you," Grandma said to Mitzie. "Tell your brother I said hello. I hope I can see you again before you head home."

Grandma turned to our server and apologized for the holdup. The young lady smiled and said no problem before taking us to our table.

"Who was that?" I asked once we were seated.

"That was Mitzie. She used to live here years ago.

She worked for the mayor for years, then one day, she decided to move and start somewhere fresh. She was thirty-five and said she was bored with her life."

I could understand that.

"That was nearly twenty years ago. She came into my shop a little over a week ago and I was so surprised to see her. I knew her mother wasn't doing well, but I didn't realize the family was called in to say good-bye." Grandma's eyes turned glassy. "Her mother died later that day."

"I'm so sorry," I said, reaching out and putting my hand on hers. "Did you know her well?"

"She was one of us. She was in our...card... playing...group." She stumbled over the words and looked at me awkwardly.

"I don't know exactly what kind of group you're in, but I know it's not a card playing group." I chuckled and looked down at the menu, letting Grandma off the hook...for now.

A waitress came and took our drink order. Grandma ordered something called champagne tea and I ordered a strawberry kiwi spritzer, whatever that was. While we waited for our drinks, I asked her about the person sitting with Mitzie.

"That's Wanda Turnbough," she said like she had something sour in her mouth.

"I couldn't help but notice you didn't even acknowledge her."

"We're not speaking at the moment," she said, flipping over her menu.

"Do you want to talk about it?" I asked hopefully.

"Nope."

Darn it.

The waitress walked up and set down our drinks, then took our order. When she walked away, I hoped that Grandma would change her mind but instead she started a conversation about a new grocery store coming in across town. I made a mental note of the woman's name and decided to see if I could figure out for myself what was going on between them.

An hour later, we were leaving the tea room and I was completely full. I'd eaten several tiny smoked salmon and cream cheese sandwiches, a salad with turkey and a sweet cranberry dressing, and French onion soup that was served in a little bread bowl. I ended the meal with an apricot and ginger scone. I had never felt so satisfied in my life.

When we got back home, I changed out of the dress and into my usual jeans and t-shirt. When I walked back into the living room, Grandma was headed outside. "The gang's sitting by the pool drinking wine. Want to join us?"

I glanced out the door and saw a group of people sitting in lawn chairs, laughing hysterically about something. I was tempted to say no, but then I had a thought—maybe I'd learn a little something, maybe they'd let something slip, or better yet, maybe

Grandma Dean would open up if she was indeed having financial problems. I'd learned over the years that wine was the lubricant of truth. So was tequila.

"Sure," I said, following her out the door.

They shouted to us as we got closer. They were an excited bunch. "Pull up a chair!"

We grabbed a lawn chair and added it to their circle. Wine glasses clinked and were passed around to us.

"This is my daughter's daughter, Nikki," Grandma Dean said.

A chorus of "hellos" rang out.

"You've already met a few of the gang," Grandma said to me. She went around the circle. "You know Lloyd." He winked at me as Grandma continued. "And of course Hattie and Irene..." They waved at me simultaneously. "And then there's Greta and Virginia." Greta smiled and Virginia lifted her glass to me.

"Were you guys out here having a party without us?" Grandma asked as she took the wine bottle and added a little more to her glass.

"We knocked on your door but no one answered." Greta fished a bag of mixed nuts out of her purse and passed it around.

"We went to The Cobbler's Tea Room for dinner," Grandma said, taking a handful of nuts out of the bag. She handed it to me, but I passed it on. I couldn't fit another thing in my stomach if I tried.

Irene looked at Lloyd. "I love that place. You should take me sometime."

Lloyd laughed a deep laugh and lowered his voice. "Okay, but if I pay, you'll owe me."

Irene giggled and I felt sick to my stomach.

"I gotta be careful," Lloyd said to her. "One of these days, I might get you pregnant."

The group laughed and I sat there trying to think of a good excuse to go back inside.

Irene put her hand on Lloyd's leg and winked. "We'll just have to be extra careful then."

Oh, Irene, I thought. *Your eggs left your cuckoo's nest a long time ago.*

"Did you see the bulletin board the nurse put up in the lobby?" I was thankful Hattie was changing the subject. "It said we had a higher STD rate than any other facility in the county. Even the local high schools!" She sat back, proudly. "Can you image that? Our Sexual Trysts Daily rate is higher than the young folks!"

I looked at Grandma. She winced and slightly shook her head at me to stay quiet. I looked at the other faces in the group to see their reactions, but no one seemed to know, or care, that Hattie had the acronym wrong. Instead, they laughed at her and poured more wine.

"All thanks to Lloyd," Virginia said, raising her glass. Everyone put their glasses to the center of the circle and shouted, "To Lloyd!"

Suddenly, Grandma's phone started beeping. She pulled it out and read a text. She looked up at the group and nodded. Quickly, everyone but Lloyd and I got up.

"Party over already, girls?" Lloyd asked, disappointed.

"Gotta run," Grandma Dean said. She looked down at me. "Don't wait up for me. I might be late."

"Where are you going?" I asked. "Do you need me to come along too?"

"No." She patted me on the shoulder. "We just have something to take care of."

A minute later, they were gone and I was left stranded with Lloyd. I looked over at him and he looked like a sad little puppy.

"Where do you think they're going?" I asked him.

"Who knows." He took a sip of wine. "They run off like that all the time and they never let me go with them." He pouted a little and pulled his silky robe across his body. I was thankful I no longer had a view of the speedos. Didn't that man ever wear clothes?

I figured this was a good time to ask if he knew anything about the lady we saw at the restaurant. "Lloyd," I asked casually. "Do you know Wanda Turnbough?"

"Yeah, she lives in four B." He eyed me suspiciously. "Why do you ask? Did you hear something? Does she want me back?"

"Um, I'm not sure." He looked disappointed again.

"We saw her at the tea room tonight and Grandma didn't talk to her. Do they not get along?"

Lloyd laughed. "Wanda's just ticked because Geraldine wouldn't let her in their little group."

"Why wouldn't she let her in?"

"You didn't hear this from me, okay?"

I nodded.

"Irene told me it's because Wanda is two years younger than Geraldine."

"So, what does that have to do with anything?"

Lloyd laughed again. "Your grandmother wants to be the youngest person in the group. She wasn't about to let Wanda take that title."

I rolled my eyes. That sounded exactly like something Grandma Dean would do.

"But don't worry," Lloyd said. "They'll get over this tiff soon enough. No one can stay mad at Geraldine for too long."

It was quiet for a minute while Lloyd and I sipped our wine and looked up at the stars.

"Lloyd," I said, pouring a little more wine in my glass and reaching over and adding a little more to his. "Have you heard anything about who might be responsible for the fire at Grandma's shop?"

He shook his head. "I have no idea. Everyone likes Geraldine."

"Do you think there's a chance that Wanda did it?"

"Wanda? Oh, no. She might be mad right now, but she would never do anything like that."

"How do you know?" I asked.

"She's too straight-laced. Everything is by the books. That's one reason why we broke up. She never wanted to have any fun."

"Okay, what about Perry Landon? Do you know him?"

"I know him as much as everybody else does, which isn't much. He mainly keeps to himself. I see him at the grocery store every once in a while. I know he hung out at the shop a lot."

"Do you think he could've done it?"

Lloyd thought about it for a minute. "I guess I don't know. I can't say for sure either way. He's a quiet fellow, a bit strange, but I don't know if he would do something like that."

I leaned back in my lawn chair and looked up at the sky. Thanks to the lights around the pool, only the brightest stars were visible. Suddenly, my curiosity got the best of me.

"So, you don't have to answer this if it's too personal..." I paused, questioning if I should ask him. "How many ladies here have you dated?"

He leaned back, a big smile overtaking his face. "All of them except your grandmother."

"All of them?" I asked, surprised.

"Yep. I think women are like fine cars. You have to ride them every once in a while or their parts stop working." He winked at me. "I've been trying to stick my wrench in Geraldine's chassis since she got here, but she won't have anything to do with it."

That was enough for me. It was my own fault for asking.

"Okayyy," I said, standing up. "I'm going to head inside. You have a good evening, Lloyd."

"Oh, come on! Not you too. Just stay out here a little longer. It's such a nice night!"

"Nope," I said, putting down my glass and walking away. For a moment, I had thought Lloyd was sweet and maybe just a little misunderstood. He quickly reminded me that I had him pegged right the first time I met him. He was creepy.

I made two mental notes as I walked into Grandma Dean's apartment: find out more about Perry Landon and stay far away from Lloyd.

10

THE NEXT MORNING, I lay in bed thinking about Perry Landon. How was I going to find out more about him? Maybe I could find out where he lived and pay him a little visit. Maybe I could bring him some donuts and apologize for making him uncomfortable at Bev's antique store. This plan had two things going for it: one, I would have an excuse to get donuts, and two, if word got back to Grandma Dean that I talked to him, and I was sure it would, I would look like the good guy this time.

I was just about ready to get out of bed when Grandma Dean came in with Kitty Purry tucked under her arm.

"Are you getting up?" she asked, ducking into the closet. "I'm having a meeting here in a few minutes and I think maybe this would be a good time for you to go outside and get some fresh air."

I rolled my eyes. She was kicking me out. Suddenly, I had a flashback to my elementary school days when I didn't want to go to school. Would the same tricks that worked on my mother work on Grandma Dean?

I listened to her rummaging through the closet and waited until she walked out carrying a tiny outfit draped over her arm.

"Do you have a stomachache?" I asked, making sure to add just the right amount of discomfort to my voice.

"No," Grandma Dean said as she sat Kitty Purry on the side of the bed. "Why?"

"I feel terrible and I was just wondering if it was something I ate."

A look of worry flashed across Grandma Dean's face and I could tell she was concentrating on her insides, searching for any sort of pain or distress. I secretly smiled. The seed had been planted.

"You know, now that you mention it, I do feel a little queasy today."

I lay back, pulling the blankets up to my chin. "I think I'm just going to rest for a while," I said as I turned to my side. "Maybe that will make me feel better. Hopefully, it's just something I ate and I'm not actually coming down with something."

I couldn't see Grandma Dean's face, but I could hear the air leave her lungs. She was worried. "I'll bring you some probiotics," she said as she carried a freshly dressed Kitty Purry out the door. "I'll be right back."

Within minutes, she was back with a supplement cocktail of ginger, vitamin C, and probiotics. She refused to leave until I took them and even then, she stood there staring at me for a minute. "I hope you're not getting sick," she finally said. "That's the last thing I need."

"I'll be fine after I rest while," I reassured her. "I just feel so weak."

She made her way to the door and turned to me before she walked out. "You rest then. I'll come and check on you when my friends leave. If you need anything in the meantime, just text me." She paused, a look of worry overtaking her face. "My meeting is... private," she said cautiously.

"Don't worry," I said, wrinkling my face like I was in pain. "I'm not going anywhere."

She stood in the doorway for a minute before finally walking out and closing the door behind her.

Now was my chance to find out what these meetings were all about.

It didn't take long for Grandma's friends to arrive. They seemed to all come at once. I could hear muffled talking, but I couldn't make anything out. There was a lot of laughter and I assumed they were just greeting each other, so no reason to get out of bed just yet.

Finally, the laughter died down and I could hear a quiet hum of voices just beyond the wall. Now they were finally getting started. I got out of bed and tiptoed across the floor. I held my breath as I slowly turned the doorknob, pulling slightly once it was completely turned.

I opened the door a crack and listened.

"Do you think she's sick? Or do you think it was bad salmon from The Cobbler's Tea Room?" I recognized Irene's voice immediately.

"I don't know," Grandma Dean replied. "But she looked terrible."

"Are you sure it's okay to have the meeting here?" Hattie asked. "She can't hear us can she?"

"No," Grandma Dean assured them. "She went right back to sleep."

"I bet you she's coming down with the stomach flu that's going around." I wasn't sure, but I thought that might have been Virginia speaking.

"You know half the county has had it," she continued. "Remember, I had it two weeks ago. I couldn't stay out of the bathroom!"

"Oh yes," Hattie chimed in. "I had it too. I nearly lost my bowels in the butter aisle at the Savemart."

I cringed at the thought.

I heard a sigh but couldn't recognize the voice that followed. "Well, I've had the opposite problem. I'm so backed up I can practically taste it."

I couldn't take anymore bowel talk. I was just about to close the door and climb back in bed when Grandma Dean spoke up. "Okay, ladies, we have a lot to discuss so we should get started."

"Do you think the cops know it was us?" Was that Hattie? Or Irene? Why were they suddenly talking so quiet?

"I don't think so," Grandma said, her voice hushed. "But I'm afraid we were a little careless. I don't want to mention names, but someone dropped something out there."

"I'm sorry. It was me. My hands were full and we were in such a hurry..." Virginia's sentence trailed off and I couldn't hear the last of it.

"What we need to discuss is what we're going to do with the money when we get it."

Grandma Dean's words made my blood freeze. In my shock, I accidentally let go of the door handle, which caused it to spin back around.

"What was that?" a worried Hattie asked.

"Probably just the cat," Grandma Dean mumbled. "But I'll go check."

I quickly and carefully closed the door then jumped in bed and pulled the covers up just as Grandma peeked her head inside. My heart was pounding in my chest as I tried to concentrate and slow my breathing.

"Nikki," I heard her say barely above a whisper. "Are you awake? I have donuts out here. Would you like one? They have sprinkles!"

Oh, that was low. Trying to trick me by using my weakness against me.

She stood in the doorway for a full minute before finally closing the door. I let out a breath and stared up at the ceiling. Lloyd had thought they were a neighborhood watch group, but I thought it was the opposite. They weren't preventing crimes; they were committing them.

11

THE NEXT HOUR and a half dragged on. I was thankful when I finally heard the front door opening and the high-pitched chatter of the women saying good-bye. Hopefully that meant Grandma Dean would be in soon to let me know that everyone had left and I was free to come out of my room.

"How are you feeling?" Grandma Dean asked a few minutes later when she peeked her head in the door.

"Much better," I said, getting out of bed. "All I needed was a little rest."

She gave me a look that said she wasn't too convinced. "Get dressed," she said as she was leaving the room. "I have some place I want to show you."

Thirty minutes later, we were in the car. "You haven't eaten yet; you must be starving." She rummaged through her purse and pulled something out. "Try one of these. You'll love it!"

I took the little package from her, hoping it was a granola bar—the kind with chocolate chips and a layer of chocolate at the bottom. I was deeply disappointed.

"What is this?" I opened the wrapper and looked at the little log that sat in my hand.

Grandma sighed. "It's a fruit and nut bar. It also has flax, pumpkin seeds, and chia seeds. It's good for you."

"Chia seeds? Like the ones that come in the little kit?"

"What kit?" I could tell she was irritated with me as she drove out of the parking lot.

"You know those kits you used to be able to order off the TV. What were they called...Chia Pets! I had a dog when I was a kid!" I looked down at the bar. It looked like bird food.

"I've never heard of such a thing," she said, looking straight ahead. "Just eat it." She glanced at me. "The wrapper is even edible!"

I let out a laugh. "I'll eat this weird bar, but there's no way I'm going to eat the wrapper!"

Grandma loosened up and laughed too. "I've never been able to get myself to eat it either."

"The bar or the wrapper," I asked her. She laughed but didn't answer my question.

It wasn't long before I noticed we were headed downtown. I started to get a sick feeling in the pit of my stomach. What was Grandma Dean up to?

"What are we doing here?" I asked as we neared her shop.

To my surprise, she drove right past it and pulled into a parking spot a block away on the other side of the street. Grandma's face lit up. "I'm here to sign the lease on my new shop! I wanted you to come too so you could see my new store!"

I was shocked. "You're signing a lease? Already? What about your other store?"

Grandma turned serious. "I have no idea when they'll hand it back over to me. I can't just sit around and do nothing while they try to figure out who started the fire."

"But what happens when they finally turn it back over to you?" I asked. "You own that part of the building, right? What will you do with two shops?"

"I've always wanted to own an old fashioned ice cream shop," she said, smiling. "Maybe I'll turn it into one of those! I could decorate it with pictures of celebrities from the past." She beamed as she told me her plans. "Or," she said, getting even more excited, "I could turn it into a little sandwich shop." She unclicked her seatbelt. "The options are endless! It could be whatever I wanted. Or whatever we wanted."

She smiled and it took me a minute to understand what she meant. When I finally got it, my heart swelled. She was saying we could open something together. I wasn't sure I wanted to commit to staying here long enough to go into business with Grandma Dean, but it made my heart happy to know she was willing to do that with me.

We got out of the car and walked up to the door of the new shop. Grandma opened the door and spoke to the man waiting for us inside. "Hey, Rog," she said, extending her hand to him.

"Good morning, Geraldine!" he said brightly. "Who's your sidekick?"

She turned to me. "This is my daughter's daughter, Nikki. Nikki, this is Roger Matthews."

I extended my hand and he took it, then pulled me in for a hug. I wasn't expecting it and I nearly fell into him. "It's nice to meet you!" he said cheerily. "I've heard a lot about you!"

I wasn't sure what to say. Not only had I never heard of him, I didn't even know until just minutes ago that Grandma was going to be leasing a store from him.

I let the two of them talk and I roamed around the store, taking everything in. I could tell right away that it had once been a hardware store. The few shelves held items long forgotten by the last tenants—a few boxes of nails, a can of motor oil, pieces of pipe. In the corner sat a sign. "Havard's Hardware." I stood there and stared at it for a minute. I used to go to school with a Havard. Kelly, I thought her name was. Or was it Shelley? I wondered if it was any relation.

Before long, I heard Roger and Grandma Dean laughing and then I heard the jingling of keys. "Take good care of her," Roger said. "If anyone can bring this place back to life, it's you!"

He left and Grandma turned to me with an excited gleam in her eyes that I knew meant I would be working the rest of the day.

"Come on!" she called, waving me toward the front of the store. "We have work to do!"

"Where are we going?"

"To my storage unit on the edge of town!"

It took nearly twenty minutes to drive to "Sinner's Self Storage." Under the name was a Bible verse, John 14:2, with the words "When you don't live like Jesus."

"What does that mean?" I asked Grandma. She laughed. "Pull it up on your phone," she said as she pulled into a parking spot in front of a storage unit.

"My phone doesn't have internet," I said as I pulled my phone out of my pocket.

Grandma Dean looked at me like I was crazy. "What do you mean your phone doesn't have Internet? Let me see it."

I handed her my phone.

"What is this?" she asked disgusted.

"It's my phone."

"You can only talk on this?"

"No, I can text too."

She gave me an "are you serious?" look. "This is a flip phone. Nobody uses these anymore!"

"Well, I use it!" I took the phone back and returned it to my pocket. I liked my little phone.

Grandma scoffed. "When we open the new antique shop, that will be the first item we put in the store." She pulled out her phone and typed in the verse. She handed it to me to read:

"My Father's house has many rooms…"

"You know, if you don't have as many rooms as Jesus, you need a storage unit…"

"I get it," I said as I handed the phone back to her.

"It confused a lot of the old people around here. Was he making fun of the Bible or was it a way to get people to read God's word? People couldn't figure it out." She laughed. "Hattie tried to get people to sign a petition to force him to change the name, but no one wanted to sign it in case it actually prompted someone to open their Bible."

Grandma got out of the car and I stood behind her and waited for her to open the storage unit's door. When she did, I couldn't believe what I saw. It was packed full of boxes. You couldn't fit another box in there if you tried.

"What is all of this stuff?" I asked.

"It's all the things I was eventually going to put in my old shop; all things that will now go in my new shop!"

She started hauling out boxes and I pointed out that they weren't all going to fit in her little car.

"Cliff Sinner is going to be here any minute. He's going to load all of this in his truck and take it to my shop." She pulled out a few more boxes, opening them to peek inside.

"Is any of this stuff going to go to Bev?" I asked.

"No," Grandma said, pulling brown packing paper out of a large box. "This is all stuff I decided to keep. I had a little bit of storage in the back of my shop," she sighed, "where the fire was started, but I kept most of my things here."

Cliff pulled up just then and jumped out of his truck. "Wow!" he said, taking a look at Grandma Dean's unit. "This is going to take more than one trip!"

Grandma laughed and patted him on the arm. "I bet you can get it done in one load!"

I helped load the truck and soon it was obvious to everyone that there was no way it was all going to fit in one load...and probably not even two.

"You go on to your shop," Cliff said to us as he closed the lift gate. "I'll deliver this one and make sure you get the rest of your boxes this afternoon."

Grandma thanked him and we drove off, back toward downtown.

"Cliff seems nice," I said as we drove along.

"He's very nice," she said. "He's the kind of guy who would do anything for anybody."

When we got back to Grandma's shop, she immediately put me to work sweeping the floors and throwing away all the junk that littered the place. It seemed to be smaller than her old shop, but it was hard for me to tell since I had never actually been in her old one—just looked at it through the busted windows on the day it went up in flames.

While I cleaned, Grandma sorted through the boxes

that Cliff dropped off in the first load. She was excited when a few of her friends stopped by to see if we'd made any progress. I stayed toward the back of the store while they chatted and listened to Grandma Dean give them her vision for her new shop. This was the happiest I had seen her since I moved there.

An hour later, Cliff was back with the second load and a bag of burgers and fries from a fast food restaurant. I was sure Grandma would turn her nose up at it, but she must have been as hungry as I was because she not only scarfed them down before me but she also finished her Diet Coke before I'd gotten halfway through mine.

"All right, ladies," Cliff said, stuffing his napkin and burger wrapper in a paper sack. "I'm off to get the third load! I think it's the last one too!"

Grandma thanked him and offered to pay for the food, but Cliff shook it off. Lloyd was right. Everyone did like Grandma in this town. I loved how everyone seemed so happy that she was getting back to work again.

With Cliff gone, we got back to work. It was quiet in the store as Grandma sorted through boxes, putting things in piles and breaking down the cardboard when each box was empty. I was making progress pulling down shelves and bagging up garbage. We were both lost in our own thoughts when Cliff barged back in the door a little while later. His entrance startled us both, and even more so when we saw the look on his face.

"Cliff," Grandma said, rushing to him. "What's wrong?"

He looked from her to me and then back to Grandma Dean again. "Geraldine, I'm so sorry."

"Sorry for what?" she asked confused.

"I...I thought I locked your storage unit, but I guess I didn't. When I got back there, everything inside was gone."

"What do you mean 'gone'? Like stolen?" I heard Grandma's voice crack a little.

Cliff shook his head. "I'm so sorry, Geraldine."

Grandma looked like she was going to faint. I rushed to her side and she pushed me away. "I'm calling Owen," she said, reaching for her phone.

Oh great, I thought. *Him.*

Grandma dialed his number and walked away, leaving Cliff and I standing by the door.

"Who would do this?" I asked, almost to myself.

"I don't know," Cliff said. "I feel so bad about this. How could I be so careless?"

"It's not your fault," I comforted him.

We were quiet for a moment. "You don't think there's any link to the fire, do you?" I asked Cliff.

He was silent and I didn't think he heard me at first. Finally, he spoke up. "I don't know. If I left the unit unlocked, anybody who drove by could've seen the padlock missing." He let out a deep sigh. "Heck, I don't even know for sure if I closed the door when I left that second time."

Okay, maybe it was his fault.

Grandma Dean returned, her face red with anger. "Owen is on his way."

Just then my phone rang. It was Joe.

For a minute, I thought about not answering, but then I thought that maybe he had some more information for me and would want me to meet him somewhere. That would give me the perfect reason to leave and avoid talking to Detective Owen.

"Hey," I answered as casually as I could. "What's up?"

"Hey, Nikki... I was just wondering if...if maybe you and I could get together for coffee or something. I hate the way things ended between us the other day and I thought..."

I cut him off. "Can you meet right now?"

He sounded surprised...and relieved.

"Yeah, uh, how about the coffee shop on Palm Breeze Drive?"

I was hoping he would pick the one downtown since I was just a few blocks away and within walking distance, but I agreed. Hopefully, Grandma Dean would let me borrow her car for a little bit. Was that too much to ask when she was in the middle of another crisis? But then I thought about it. Most likely she would be stuck here talking to the police for a while anyway. I might even be back before they left. Ugh, I hoped not.

I told him I would meet him there in fifteen

minutes. I asked Grandma Dean if I could borrow her keys and she handed them to me like she was in a daze.

"Cliff, can you stay with her until the police get here?" I asked him. "I have to meet someone really quick. I'll be back as soon as I can."

"I won't leave her side," he promised me.

As I walked out the door, Detective Owen was pulling up. We made eye contact briefly and I tried to hurry to Grandma's car before he got out of his. Unfortunately, he was faster than I was.

"Nikki," he called out to me just as I was opening the car door. "Do you have a minute?"

I stopped and gave him my best dirty look. "What do you want?" I asked coldly.

"I...um...I'm sorry about what happened the other day at the coffee shop. I was just doing my job, but..." He stopped and looked at me sincerely. "I didn't mean to upset you."

Two apologies from two hot guys in one day. Grandma Dean may be having a terrible day, but mine seemed to be going pretty well.

"Don't worry about it," I said, forgiving him. "Just please take care of my grandma. She's pretty shook up over this last incident."

"I will," he promised.

I got in the car and watched him walk into Grandma's new shop. Suddenly, I wanted to forget about Joe and follow Owen inside.

I put my head back on the seat. This was how I got

myself into so much trouble with guys. This was how I ended up with so many ex-husbands. I shamed myself for being so weak and pulled out of the parking space. Suddenly, something got my attention from across the street, or rather, someone. Perry Landon stood on the curb staring at me. Why was he there? Why was he watching me?

12

THE PALM BREEZE Coffee Shop looked more like a snow cone hut than a coffee shop. It was painted bright blue with white trim and had two large palm trees out front. Adirondack chairs with little tables sitting between them were set up on a side patio.

I looked around and felt very out of place. The coffee shop was packed with tan girls in flip-flops, short shorts, and high ponytails. This must have been where the popular girls went to get their coffee.

I found Joe surrounded by a group of extra perky double-Ds. I watched him for a moment before I went over and claimed him. Even though he was clearly enjoying the attention from the beautiful women, he seemed shy and a little awkward. I knew right then that he was a one-woman kind of guy.

"Hey, Joe!" I said as I approached him. He smiled and I saw his face flush a little.

"Excuse me, ladies," he said, turning sideways and squeezing past them.

I couldn't help but see them look me up and down, clearly unimpressed. I could've been offended, but honestly, I didn't know what men saw in me either. I didn't have amazing features or a to-die-for body. And I could never get my hair in one of those perfect, sleeked back ponytails.

We ordered our drinks and took a seat on the patio.

"So," I said, removing the little paper umbrella that was sticking out of my coconut frappe, "what did you want to talk about?"

Joe sighed and sat his drink on the table. He leaned closer to me. "I feel really bad about the other day. I don't know what came over me. One minute, I was irritated with my brother; the next, I was embarrassed by my cousin Eddie; and the next, I was kissing you." He shook his head and looked down at his shoes. "I was out of line and I'm sorry."

He looked so cute when he felt bad.

"Oh, don't worry about it," I said, smiling. "I've had much worse things happen to me." I gave him a wink and he straightened back up in his chair. I could almost see the guilt slip away.

Part of me wanted to explain my situation to him, but part of me didn't even know where to start. I decided instead to change the subject.

"So the person who set fire to Grandma Dean's shop might have struck again."

Joe's face turned serious. "What happened?"

I told him about the second shop and Cliff Sinner delivering the boxes and then how the last load was stolen before he made it back to the storage unit. "Who do you think would do something like that?" I asked him.

He shook his head. "I have no idea."

"I have a bad feeling about that Perry Landon guy," I said, stirring my drink. "I saw him when I was leaving Grandma's shop today. He was standing across the street, staring at me."

"That guy's harmless," Joe said, picking up his glass and taking a drink. "This stuff is crazy good. Wanna try it? It's mango iced tea."

I thought about it for a minute and decided to pass. I was too irritated at the moment to share a drink.

"How can you say he's harmless?" I asked him. "He was always at Grandma's shop before it went up in flames and now he's across the street from her new one spying on her!"

"You don't know if he was spying on her." His voice softened when he realized I was upset. "Look, Nikki, I know you want to figure out who is doing this to Geraldine, but I really think Perry is innocent. He's a quiet guy and I think he's just misunderstood." He could tell I wasn't buying it. "The police will catch the criminal," he soothed. "Owen is a good detective. He'll figure it all out."

I scoffed. "Yeah, right. I have zero faith in the guy."

That wasn't necessarily true, but my emotions were getting the best of me at the moment.

Joe's phone started beeping and he looked at it. "Sorry," he said, stuffing it back in his pocket and standing up. "I've gotta go. There's a fire and it's all hands on deck."

My blood went cold. "Please tell me it's not downtown."

He laughed and extended his hand to help me up from my chair. "No, it's at a factory on the other side of town."

I should've felt relieved, but for some reason I didn't. We said our good-byes and I got back in Grandma Dean's car. I felt so uneasy. What was happening in this town? What was happening with Grandma Dean?

As soon as I got in the car, I got a text. When I tried to read it, I spilled my frappe on my pants.

"Crap," I said as I put it in the cup holder. I glanced at my phone and saw that it was from Grandma Dean:

"Got a ride home from Detective Owen. Will see you when you get here."

I put the phone on my lap and reached for the glove compartment, hoping for some napkins. When I opened it, something black fell out. I left it lying on the floor for a minute while I grabbed a package of handy wipes and went to work wiping off my hands and pants and then the center console, which I realized also had drops of frappe on it. I sure could make a mess.

With everything cleaned up, I returned the package of wipes to the glove compartment and leaned over to pick up the item that had fallen on the floor. It looked like a black knitted hat, which surprised me since this was Florida...and that wasn't a hat I pictured Grandma Dean wearing. I unfolded it to get a better look and my heart nearly stopped beating. It wasn't just a regular knitted hat, it was a ski mask. I quickly shoved it back in the glove compartment and sat up straight in my seat. What had Grandma Dean gotten herself into?

By the time I got to Grandma Dean's house, I was furious. I grabbed the ski mask before I stormed inside. I was tired of her lies—or at the very least, her half-truths. I wanted answers.

When I walked in, she was in the living room sorting through her mail. I threw the ski mask on the coffee table in front of her.

"What is this?" I demanded.

Her face went pale and she stammered for a moment. "It...it appears to be a hat of some sort."

"I know what it is!" I shouted. "What I want to know is, why was it in your car?"

She looked up, but remained silent.

I couldn't take it anymore. I burst into tears, partly out of anger and partly out of frustration.

"Nikki," she said, patting the couch next to her. "Come sit with me."

"You're guilty of something! What is it?! Did you burn your own shop down for the insurance money like Owen thinks you did? Did you burn down the factory across town too? Is that your thing? You and your little group, you all look innocent but you're really planning your next crime!"

Her face turned to stone for a moment and then she burst into laughter. "Nikki, please come sit with me. I'll tell you everything. It's not what you think!"

I stood across from her and refused to sit down. Why was she laughing? This wasn't funny. This was serious.

She sighed and picked up the ski mask. "I wear this from time to time when the girls and I..." she paused and looked up at me. "Are you sure you don't want to sit?"

"No. I'm fine. Now go on."

She cleared her throat. "There are small crimes that are committed in this community and the girls and I don't feel like the police take them seriously." She looked up at me like she had just explained everything in detail and was finished with her story.

I gave her a look to let her know that she hadn't.

"Do you want me to spell it out for you?" She sounded irritated.

"Yes, I do."

"Fine, Nikki. We patrol the streets at night and take matters into our own hands. We meet a few times a week and talk about things that are happening in our community and then we go out and take care of it. Sometimes that means doing a good deed for someone and sometimes that means catching a criminal in the act. But no matter what we do, it's done in secrecy."

"Why were you talking about getting money at your last meeting?"

"I knew that noise wasn't the cat." She shot me a dirty look. "Sometimes, we get rewards for tipping the police or for turning in a suspect. We use that money to do something nice for someone in the community that needs it."

I stood there thinking it over. If what she was saying was true, then she was a modern day superhero.

I finally walked over and sat next to her on the couch. She looked so tiny to me all of a sudden. I didn't like the idea of her out there catching bad guys and putting herself in harm's way. She must have read my mind.

"It's okay, Nikki," she said, her voice soft. "We're careful. That's why I have one of these, so people don't recognize me. We all wear one." She sighed and picked up the ski mask. "Unfortunately, I'm afraid someone we turned in found out my identity and now they're trying to get back at me."

I gasped. It all made sense now. Someone was retaliating against her for turning them in. "Do you have any idea who it is? Does Detective Owen know about all of this?"

"He knows as much as he needs to know," Grandma said, putting the ski mask down. "And no, I'm not sure who started the fire or stole my things. But believe me, we're going to find out one way or another. The Glock Grannies always get our man...or woman...and one time, an alligator wearing a wedding dress."

For a moment, I thought she was joking about the alligator until I saw her get lost in her thoughts and shudder. There was a lot more to Geraldine Dean than I originally thought, and I had a feeling we were just scratching the surface.

13

―――――――――――――

IT ONLY TOOK a few days to get the shop in order, and
we couldn't have done it without Cliff Sinner's help.
The three of us had a system: I cleaned, Grandma Dean
unpacked the boxes, and Cliff hauled away the trash
and empty boxes. Cliff and I both helped Grandma
Dean set up the shop to her liking and when it was
finished, we stood back to admire our hard work. It
looked like an antique shop.

"There's a lot more I'd like to do," Grandma Dean
said, rubbing her lower back. "But I think this is good
for now."

"It looks real nice," Cliff said, looking around. "You
ought to be real proud of yourself for getting it up and
running so quickly."

"Well, I couldn't have done it without you…or
Nikki."

I was exhausted. As we turned out the lights and

locked up, I said a silent prayer that Grandma Dean's grand opening tomorrow would go off without a hitch and whoever was trying to sabotage her would stay far, far away. I shuddered thinking about it. Both Grandma Dean and Joe had a lot of faith that Owen would catch the person behind all the trouble, but I was afraid they were all looking at the wrong person.

"OH!" Grandma said just before she opened the store for the first time. "I forgot about the sign! Cliff, would you hang it out front for me?"

"Sure thing," he said, putting down the rag he had been using to dust off the furniture.

Grandma disappeared in the back of the store and came back carrying the sign. As she handed it to Cliff, I got a glimpse of it for the first time. It was teal with big white letters that said, "Junk in the Trunk." All this time I had been there and I had never even asked Grandma what the name of her store was, and now that I knew, I couldn't help but laugh.

"That's the name of your store? Junk in the Trunk?"

"Yes," she said proudly, handing the sign to Cliff. "I've tried to get one of the Kardashians to visit the store, but so far no one has replied to my letters. But one day they will. I just know it!"

Cliff disappeared out the front door and Grandma

looked at me and took a deep breath. "Are you ready?" she asked.

I nodded.

"Oh, here!" she said, handing me her phone. "Take a picture of me turning the sign to "open." I'll post it on my social media pages later today!"

She handed me the phone and I took a picture. Then we had to redo it several times because Grandma wasn't happy with first the angle and then the lighting. Finally, we had a picture she was happy with.

The sign had barely stopped swaying after it had been flipped before Grandma got her first visitors to the store. Hattie and Irene stopped by with coffee and donuts. I was starting to really like them.

The rest of the day was more of the same. Virginia came by in the afternoon and Greta came by shortly after. Before we closed for the day, Mitzie McCreedy and the grumpy old lady, Wanda Turnbough, came in with flowers in a pale green vase. Mitzie was all smiles, but Wanda still had the same sour look she had at the tea room.

Just as Grandma was about to flip the sign to "closed," Perry Landon opened the door.

"Tell him we're closing," I whispered to Grandma Dean.

"I can't do that," she whispered back. "That would be rude! He'll just be in here a few minutes."

Grandma made light conversation with him and then told me she was running to the back to take care of a few things. I watched him like a hawk as he went through the box of odds and ends that Grandma had put out especially for him. He looked up at me a few times and smiled, but I kept up with my steely glare. I wanted him to know I was on to him.

After a few minutes, he came up to the counter and sat down the items in his hand—a glass doorknob, a small matchbook, some leather buttons, and a handful of tacks that had a little pink flower on the head.

"Those are some interesting items," I said as I rang them up. "What are you going to do with them?"

He suddenly seemed nervous and refused to make eye contact. "Just collecting things," he said, staring at them.

I gave him his total and he reached in his pocket, pulling out a bunch of balled up dollar bills. He sat three of them on the counter, scooped up his items, stuffed them in his pocket, and walked away.

"Hey," I called after him. "What about your change?"

He acted like he didn't hear me and made a beeline for the door.

When Grandma emerged from the back a few minutes later, I told her what happened. "There's something that isn't right with that man," I said to her after I had finished the story.

Grandma Dean laughed it off as usual. "Oh, he's harmless."

That was what I kept hearing, but it wasn't what I believed.

"WHAT'S IN THE BAG?" Grandma asked on our ride home.

"Oh," I said, reaching for it. "There were a few things from your store I wanted to take home."

Grandma raised an eyebrow. "Stealing from me on the first day?" she said jokingly.

"No," I said, suddenly remembering the basket in my room that I needed to return to Bev…and the plates I still needed to return to the coffee shop. "I just thought these would look cute in my room. You keep telling me I should personalize my room a little, and I thought these things would look nice in there."

I pulled out an old, metal lantern that was rusted on the edges. It was white and looked like it had been weathered by the sea. There was something about it that I loved.

"That's beautiful," Grandma said, driving away from downtown. "That will look great in your room."

Next I pulled out a black lacquered box with a thin red dragon painted all along the bottom half. A sharp, metal ledge separated the top and bottom. Grandma made a face.

"You don't like this one?" I asked her.

"It's not really my style." She shrugged.

"I liked it because it's big enough I could keep papers and mail in," I said as I reached for the last thing in the bag. "This next one is my favorite," I said to her. I pulled out a peach-colored bowl with a little blue bird perched on the edge. I held it in both hands like it was the most valuable thing in the world.

"Now, that's pretty," Grandma said.

I smiled as I looked at it. There was something about that little blue bird that stole my heart. It was so delicate and tiny, and yet the details in its little face gave it a personality.

As I carefully returned my little treasures to the bag, I thought about Perry Landon. Was he really just collecting things? Or was he there today to scope out the place? A chill ran up my spine. I had to find a way to talk to him, but how?

"I'M HAVING one of my meetings in a little bit," Grandma said when we walked through her front door. She sat her purse on the table and walked over to make some tea.

I sighed. "Are you kicking me out or can I stay in my room if I promise not to eavesdrop?"

Grandma stirred in some sugar. "I was thinking maybe you could join us today."

My mouth fell open in shock. "Really?"

"Well," she said, putting some crackers and cheese on a plate for her guests, "you already know what we're up to, and who knows? Maybe some young blood will be good for us." She laughed. "And a young body.

There've been a few times we've had to scale a wall or two, and let me just say that it didn't turn out very well."

I could imagine.

I ran to the bathroom and when I was in there, the ladies started to arrive. As I washed my hands, I tried to prepare myself for what one of Grandma Dean's meetings would be like. Would we really take off afterward, chasing a villain in the night? Would I get my own ski mask? Maybe a fake name?

When I walked back in to the kitchen, I was met with a table full of dirty looks.

"What's she doing here?" Hattie asked.

"I thought she could join us," Grandma said, sitting a bowl of fruit salad on the table.

"Are you nuts?" Irene shouted. "She can't be in on one of our…card playing meetings!"

"Calm down," Grandma Dean warned. "She already knows what we're up to. She found my ski mask."

Several of the ladies gasped.

"She promises she won't tell a soul what we're up to, don't you, Nikki?"

I nodded. "I promise."

The ladies didn't look convinced.

"I say we make her take a blood oath," Virginia said, narrowing her eyes at me.

I looked at Grandma for help.

"You're not going to slice her open, Virginia.

Remember what happened when you did that to Betty?"

The group gasped and shook their heads.

"That was terrible," Greta said, her face as white as a sheet.

"That wasn't my fault," Virginia said defensively. "She should've told me she was on blood thinners!"

I looked around the room. I knew all of the ladies at this point and not one of them was named Betty. What happened to the poor old woman? Did she bleed to death? Decide she didn't want to be a part of a group that made her nearly bleed out just to join? I'd have to ask Grandma Dean about it later.

"Okay," Hattie said, "I have a better idea. In order for Nikki to be a member of this group, she has to get her eyebrows done."

I laughed, thinking she was joking. I looked around the table, expecting everyone else to be laughing too, but they weren't. Instead, they were nodding in agreement.

"You have to be joking," I finally said.

"Dear…" Greta placed her hand over mine. "I didn't want to say anything, but your eyebrows cast a shadow on your face and it makes your nose look terribly long. If you'd just cut those things back, your whole face would brighten up!" She smiled at me like she had somehow just given me a compliment instead of an insult.

I looked up at Grandma Dean.

"It's true," she said matter-of-factly.

"I think I'd rather take my chances with Virginia and the blood oath," I said under my breath.

"Trust me," Greta whispered to me. "You don't want to do that."

"All right, fine! I'll join your little group and I'll get my eyebrows done. Are you happy now?"

A chorus of cheers rang out and I sunk into my chair. It had better be worth it.

"Okay," Grandma said, taking charge of the group. "We have a lot to discuss, so let's get started. The first thing we need to figure out is what we're going to do with the money from our last...apprehension." She glanced at me and then at the others, clearly sending out a silent signal for them to keep quiet about something. They didn't catch on. Instead, they started laughing. It started out as a low giggle that they tried to stifle by putting their hands over their mouths. Within minutes, it had turned into full blown, hysterical laughter.

"What's so funny?" I asked, already laughing even though I had no idea what was happening.

"Nothing," Grandma said sternly. "I can't believe you ladies are so immature!"

Another round of laughter rang out.

"Oh come on," Hattie laughed. "You have to admit, it's funny."

"I don't have to admit anything." Grandma was clearly angry, but the ladies didn't seem to care.

"What happened?" I begged. "Someone tell me!"

Grandma gave me a stern look.

"Hey," I replied, "if I'm going to get my eyebrows done to be in this group, then I deserve to know what's going on."

"Fine," Grandma said, crossing her arms. "But I'm not telling the story."

"I'll tell it!" Irene burst from her chair. "It was a night just like tonight…"

"It was four nights ago," Grandma said, rolling her eyes.

"Hush! I'm telling the story!" Irene leaned forward and became animated again. "We were out on the streets looking for a perp, but not just any perp, the scumbag Peeping Tom that had terrorized our precious town for nearly three weeks."

"As usual," Greta butted in, "the police weren't doing anything about it. We had to take matters into our own hands."

Irene cleared her throat to let Greta know she wasn't done telling the story. "We were all hanging out by the pool when we got a tip that he struck again on Seashore Drive."

I looked over at Grandma Dean. "Was this the night we were all outside and you guys had to leave so quickly?"

Grandma nodded, her arms still tightly folded across her chest.

"Anyway," Irene continued. "We parked a few blocks

away and put on our ski masks. We were slinking through the neighborhood looking for him, when all of a sudden Virginia sees him looking in a window across the street."

We all looked at Virginia, who was sitting there proudly. "I have good eyesight, possibly the best in the group."

Grandma let out a "hmph" and Irene continued. "We all stood there frozen. We hadn't actually expected to see him! We hadn't even had a chance to come up with a plan yet! Before any of us could react, Geraldine takes off running toward the house!"

The laughter started to pick up again.

"She runs right up to the man, grabs him by the wonker, and leads him to the sidewalk!"

The women broke out in laughter as I sat there in shock and looked at Grandma Dean. "You did what?"

"I meant to grab him by the hand," she said, her face bright red. "I didn't realize his hand was…"

Irene was bent over laughing and had to hold onto the table to steady herself. "Geraldine's screaming, 'Get the car! Get the car!' and instead, we're just standing there paralyzed by the sight!"

"Why didn't you just let go when you realized what it was?" I asked.

"I wasn't about to let him get away!" Grandma Dean said it like I had just suggested the most ridiculous thing ever. "Especially if he was standing outside people's windows doing *that*."

"So what happened?" I asked the group. "Did someone get the car?"

"Virginia finally did," Irene said, still laughing.

"So you just stood there on the sidewalk holding onto his..."

"Wonker," Irene yelled out.

"You did that until Virginia came back with the car?"

Grandma's face was a deep red, nearly purple. I wasn't sure if it was from embarrassment or anger. "Yes," she finally said. "Though by the time Virginia pulled up, there wasn't much to hold onto."

The ladies burst into laughter again and this time, Grandma Dean joined them. "It was horrible," she admitted. "I think I washed my hands a hundred times that night."

"Did he just stand there the whole time?" I still couldn't believe the story.

"I think he was as shocked as the rest of us," Greta said, shaking her head. "That is a night none of us will forget!"

"Even when I finally succumb to dementia, that night will still be perfectly etched in my mind," Hattie laughed. "No amount of mental deterioration will save me from that image!"

"Back to the matter at hand..." Grandma tried to say, but the comment only elicited more laughs. "No pun intended," she added. "We need to figure out what to do with our reward money."

"I think we should give it to the young mom in town that just had triplets. Can you imagine the diapers they'll go through?" Irene tried to picture it. "I had three kids, but they were all spaced out. I can't imagine what I would've done if I had them all at the same time!"

"I like that idea," Hattie agreed. "Her name is Bethany and she goes to my church. I could slip it in her purse with a little note next Sunday."

Everyone agreed and it looked like the meeting was going to be adjourned. I looked at Grandma Dean. "Are you going to talk about the possible connection between the fire and someone you turned in?" I whispered.

Greta overheard. "I don't think there is a connection. I think it was Perry."

Finally! Someone else in this town who didn't think he was just misunderstood.

Grandma Dean rolled her eyes. "Perry didn't do it. I'm sure of it."

"Then who did?" I demanded. "You have to have some idea!"

The room was quiet for the first time since the ladies arrived. They all looked at me like I was a toddler throwing a tantrum in a restaurant. "Well, who do you think is involved?" I asked Irene.

She looked at me like she didn't want to answer. "I really don't know," she finally said.

I looked at Hattie. "What about you?" She shrugged.

"Well, I agree with Greta," Virginia said. "I think it was Perry."

So they were split down the middle if Grandma didn't vote.

"We've gone over it a thousand times," Grandma said, pouring herself some more tea. "This is one case we haven't been able to figure out...yet."

"Well," Virginia said, standing up. "We're not going to figure it out tonight. Maybe he'll strike again and leave us some clues next time."

The rest of the ladies stood up and grabbed their purses before walking to the door. They turned and looked at me as I sat there, picking through the fruit salad.

"What?" I asked them, feeling suddenly self-conscious.

"Are you coming or what?" Virginia asked.

I sat there confused for a moment. "Where are we going?"

Grandma Dean walked over to me and pulled me from the chair. "You're getting your eyebrows done, remember?"

"Now?" I asked in surprise.

"Now," Virginia answered.

I stood there for a minute trying to figure out what I had gotten myself into. But then I thought back to the story of Grandma catching the "perp" and I laughed. Whatever pain lay ahead with my eyebrows was worth being able to hear that story.

14

"Are you almost ready?" Grandma's voice rang out from the kitchen while I stood in front of the bathroom mirror admiring my now delicate eyebrows. I had been against getting my brows done, but I had to admit, Grandma and her group were right. It really did brighten my face.

"Almost," I shouted through the bathroom door.

"I think I'll just drop you off and you can open the store," Grandma said as we were heading out the door that morning. "I'll run down to the coffee shop and get us some coffee."

"And cinnamon rolls?" I asked hopefully.

Grandma sighed. "You and your carbs! We need to break you of that."

I rolled my eyes.

Grandma Dean stopped and looked me over. "You're really coming together," she said proudly, like I was a project she was working on...which I probably was. "Now if I can just get you to tame that hair and wear some lip gloss."

"Ha!" I laughed. "You have a better chance of that happening than me giving up carbs!"

A few minutes later, she had dropped me off in front of her shop. It was eight in the morning and there was an unusual chill in the air. I fumbled with the keys for a minute and finally made my way in.

The shop was pitch black, so I reached for the light switch and turned on the lights. I also pulled back the newly hung curtains—teal with white polka dots—to let in the sunlight. I had thought it was unusual to hang curtains in a shop window, but Grandma Dean was right. It did give the place a cozy, at home feel.

I spun around, ready to put my bag on the counter and get the shop ready to open, when something made my heart stop. A man's shoe lay in the middle of the floor a few feet from the counter. I didn't remember that being there yesterday.

I walked over and picked it up, and then I saw the most disturbing thing I had ever seen in my life. The owner of the shoe was a few feet away, dead on the ground with a hole in his head. I let out a scream and fumbled for my phone to call 911. "A man is dead!" I screamed into the phone when the dispatcher answered. "It's Perry Landon! Perry Landon is dead!"

When Grandma got to her store, her face was pale and she was shaking nearly as bad as I was. I was standing outside talking to Detective Owen. He had already called Grandma Dean and told her what happened so she wouldn't be shocked when she pulled up and saw that her store was surrounded by police cars.

"What happened to him?" she asked Owen, fighting back tears.

"Nikki found him," he said solemnly. "He was already dead."

"But how?" Grandma Dean asked.

Detective Owen leaned closer to her. "This is just between us right now, but it looks like he took his own life."

Grandma gasped and covered her mouth as a tear slipped down her face.

"He had a note in his hand. He admitted to the whole thing—the fire, the stolen boxes. He said he'd been sneaking in your shop at night and taking things for a while now." He looked at Grandma, his brows furrowed. "Did you have any idea what he was doing?"

Grandma looked at me and then at the ground.

"Grandma Dean! Did you know Perry was breaking in to your old shop?"

"I didn't know for sure," she finally said. "I had a feeling someone was. Things were moved around occasionally and sometimes the back door was unlocked when I knew I had locked everything up the night before."

"Why didn't you ever say anything?" I asked. "Or call the police?"

"Nothing was ever taken," she said defensively. "And I was never positive it was him." She looked at Detective Owen. "But why would he have started the fire? And why would he kill himself over it?"

Owen's face flushed a little and he cleared his throat. He suddenly looked uncomfortable.

"The note said he was obsessed with you." Before he could say anymore, Owen was called away.

Grandma Dean turned to me as Owen walked away. "Obsessed with me? Did you see the note?"

"It was in his hands," I said, picturing the moment I walked over and saw him. "I let the police take it from him and I read it over their shoulder."

"What exactly did it say?'

I let out a long breath. "It's just like Owen said. And at the end, he said he was sorry he hurt you."

"I just can't believe it," she said, wiping the tears from her face. "I can't believe Perry would kill himself."

For some reason, I couldn't believe it either.

Detective Owen walked back over to us, his face serious and his voice deep. "I think you two should come with me."

Grandma was indignant. "Oh no you're not! You're not arresting us! We had nothing to do with this. It was bad enough when I was suspected of arson. I'm not about to let you arrest me for murder!"

Owen let out a little laugh. "Geraldine, I'm not

arresting you or Nikki. I have some officers at Perry's house right now and they found something I think you should see."

"Oh," Grandma Dean said, trying to regain her composure. "You should have started off with that."

Perry lived in the middle of town in a tiny light blue house with white shutters. The yard was immaculate— flowers carefully pruned, bushes all the same size, perfectly straight edging along the sidewalks. The inside, however, was a different story.

"Watch your step," Officer Garcia warned when we walked in. "It's practically a death trap in here."

The officer walked us through the dark, little house. Each room was full of boxes, trash, and clothes. Perry was a hoarder. Garcia led us to a back bedroom, and even though the room was a fairly good size, there was very little room for the four of us to stand.

"It's in there, sir." Officer Garcia motioned for Owen to open a closet door. Owen squeezed past us and opened it. His jaw dropped a little and his body went stiff.

"What is it?" Grandma Dean and I asked at the same time.

He stood aside and we inched forward to peek inside. We couldn't believe our eyes.

The closet was completely void of clothes. The only thing in there was a table that had been pushed up against the wall. Candles with hardened wax that had dripped down their sides were lined up in a row at the back. In front of them were odds and ends—a hairbrush, a tube of lipstick, a napkin.

But it was what was hanging above the table that gave us chills: a large picture of Grandma made out of all the tiny little items he had been purchasing from her shop. Buttons, earrings, paper clips, sequins—they all came together in a collage to create her portrait. If it hadn't been so creepy, it would've been beautiful.

Grandma took a step forward. "These are my things," she said quietly, pointing to the items on the table. She looked up at Detective Owen. "He really was obsessed with me."

The ride back to Grandma's shop was a silent one. Grandma Dean looked outside, lost in her own thoughts. It started to rain and I watched the water slide down the window, some drops colliding with others, others landing at the same time and chasing each other to the bottom of the window.

When Detective Owen pulled up in front of the shop, he finally spoke. "I'm really sorry about all of this, Geraldine. We'll get everything cleaned up and you'll be able to reopen in no time. We'll also wrap up the investigation in your other shop. You'll have access to that one by the end of the week."

"I'm not opening either one," she said, still looking out the window. "At least not for a while."

Detective Owen nodded like he understood and got out of the car, opening Grandma's door so she could get out too.

We heard yelling from behind us and turned to see Hattie and Irene running across the street toward us. "We just heard what happened!" Hattie said, pulling Grandma in for a hug. "Are you okay?"

Grandma shrugged. She was clearly not okay.

"What are you going to do now?" Irene asked.

Grandma Dean sighed and looked at me. "I think Nikki and I are going to take a little vacation, get away from all of this for a while."

GRANDMA BOOKED us a room at a spa hotel about thirty minutes up the coast. We were packed and headed that way within the hour. Grandma Dean sent Detective Owen a text to let him know where we were staying, in case he had any more information or needed something from us.

The light drizzle continued as we left town.

"I can't believe this has happened," she said solemnly. "Poor Perry."

The windshield wipers tried to move across the window, the rubber scraping against the glass in a noise more annoying than nails on a chalkboard.

"Grandma, there was something weird about Perry. I pointed it out to Owen, but he seemed to shrug it off."

Grandma's eyebrows perked up. "What was it?"

"He had cuts on his hands...both of them."

Grandma shrugged it off. "That could've been from anything," she said, turning back to the road.

"But they were clean and straight." I paused, thinking about how ridiculous I sounded. Grandma was right—he could've gotten them from anywhere.

BY THE TIME we checked into the resort, it was nearly lunchtime but neither of us were hungry.

"What do you want to do?" Grandma asked, looking through a brochure.

I looked at her for a minute. She looked exhausted and troubled.

"Should we get a massage?" she asked. "Maybe one of these other spa treatments?" She handed the brochure to me.

I took it and looked it over. Chemical peels, cold laser facials, micro needling—all things I was sure would appear on a brochure from an overseas terrorist training camp. Not exactly the way I wanted to spend an already stressful day.

"Wanna go to the beach?" I asked. "Maybe we could just relax for a while. The rain stopped and the sun is out."

Grandma perked up. "That's exactly what we need!" She looked at me skeptically. "Did you bring a swimsuit?"

"I have a pair of shorts and a t-shirt," I said, dreading what was coming next.

"Nikki, this isn't summer camp for fat kids. You need a real swimsuit! We'll go down to the little shop by the lobby and buy one."

I saw that little shop when we were checking in and there was no way I was going to wear any of those so-called swimsuits. I was sure even Kitty Purry's swimsuit had more material than those did.

Before I could object, Grandma Dean was already on to the next, even more disturbing topic of conversation.

"Now," she said, putting her suitcase on the bed. "Don't freak out, but we need to have a serious conversation before we head to the beach."

I cringed. *Please don't let this be a conversation about bikini waxing.*

She opened her suitcase and pulled out what looked like a paint sprayer. "You need a quick tan."

"I don't need a tan!" I objected. "I'm fine how I am!"

"Nikki, you're so white that if we turn off the lights, people will still see you."

Ouch.

"I don't care. I'm not letting you spray me with that."

Grandma Dean's face fell and for a minute, I felt bad. She'd had a rough day. If spraying me with some brown paint made her feel better, shouldn't I let her do it? I looked at the sprayer and all the tubes and bottles

Grandma had pulled out of her bag. Nope. I couldn't do it.

"How about I wear lip gloss instead?" I suggested hopefully.

Grandma thought about it for a minute. "Well, I guess it's better than nothing."

We made our way down to the little shop and flipped through the bikinis, which I turned down no matter how "cute" Grandma Dean thought they were. Finally, we came to a rack in the corner that had three one-piece swimsuits. One was black and two had a vibrant tropical theme in oranges and pinks. Grandma handed me the black one, but of course I liked the colorful ones.

I tried on the black one and looked in the mirror. Not bad. With my eyebrows done, a little bit of lip gloss, and the cute swimsuit, I could almost go out there with all the other beach-goers and not completely hate myself.

I bought it then we ran upstairs to change. Grandma Dean stepped out of the bathroom in her 1950s style swimsuit. It was a flattering cut in red with white polka dots. She looked adorable with her sunglasses on top of her head. At over seventy years old, her legs still looked better than mine. She had the perfect tan, which seemed to hide any imperfections, and for a second, I thought about giving in and letting her spray me down.

When we got to the beach, we put our towels on

loungers that faced the water. Someone came over and asked if we wanted an umbrella, but we decided we'd rather lie in the sun.

I lay there and closed my eyes, listening to the waves lap the shore. I could hear seagulls and occasionally people talking, but for the most part it felt like it was just me and the water. The air smelled sweet with the random scent of dead fish and the sun felt warm on my skin. For just a moment, I thought I could forget the awful things that had happened that day, but images of Perry, dead on the floor in Grandma's shop, filled my mind.

I looked over at Grandma and she was already asleep, evident by the low hum of her breathing. I couldn't believe how awful she had looked on the ride here. I had never seen her like that. She hadn't even reapplied her lipstick before she got out of the car to walk up to the resort. That was how you could judge if Grandma Dean was okay or not—was she wearing lipstick?

I turned my face back toward the sky and closed my eyes. I let the sun melt away my worries and stress. I could feel my muscles relaxing and my breathing grow shallow. Just as I was about to succumb to sleep, I had an image of Perry's hands. I bolted upright. I knew what would cause that! And it wasn't something he could've done on his own.

"Grandma!" I screamed. She flew out of the lounger and landed on her feet, her arms out like she was ready to use karate on whoever was standing next to her.

"It's okay," I said, grabbing her arms. "We have to go back to town. I know what happened to Perry!"

I explained everything to her on the way to town. "Remember that box I took from your shop?" I asked. "There were two of them on the shelf. I took the one that had scuffed edges and I left the one that was in better shape. They had a metal ledge that went all the way around it. If Perry was holding that and someone ripped it out of his hands, it would've sliced through them and left marks just like the ones I saw on him."

"Let's go see if that box is still in the shop," Grandma said. "If it's not, then it proves Perry wasn't alone last night."

We parked down the street and entered through the back of the shop from the alley.

"This place is still a crime scene," Grandma said as we walked in. "So don't touch anything."

We left the lights off and used the flashlight on Grandma's phone to guide us to the front of the store.

"The boxes were over here," I said, pointing to the right.

We walked over and sure enough, the second box was missing.

"What would someone want with that box?" Grandma asked. "Did you look at the one you took home? Was there anything special about it?"

"Nothing," I said. "It was lined with red silk... Do you think there was something hidden underneath it?"

"I don't know." Grandma stood there for a minute, thinking things over. "You know, I think I have another one of those in the back."

We made our way to the back where she had a few boxes stacked in the corner. She flipped the light on. "There aren't any windows so no one will be able to see from outside that the light's on." She opened a box. "Yes! I remember now! There were three boxes, but I didn't see any reason to put all three out. I put two on the shelf and then held this other one back. I figured if the others sold, I'd put it out, otherwise I'd give them all to Bev to sell in her shop."

She took out the third box that matched mine. "Where did you get these?" I asked. "Were they from an estate sale?"

Grandma Dean shook her head. "I can't remember. Sometimes people drop things off at the shop..." She looked at me and we both had the same thought. Someone wanted it back.

We held our breath as Grandma lifted the lid from the box. Our eyes went wide when we saw the folded papers inside. I took out the top one and opened it, leaning close to Grandma Dean so we could both read it.

"Well, I'll be," Grandma whispered. "Looks like we've solved our little mystery."

"I'll take that," came a voice from behind us. We

spun around and came face to face with the last person either of us wanted to see at the moment.

Mitzie McCreedy.

She snatched the paper from me and waved it in one hand while she waved a gun in the other.

"How could you do it?" Grandma asked her. "How could you kill Perry?"

Mitzie laughed nervously. "The same way I'm going to kill the two of you—with my eyes closed, so I don't have to actually see it."

"You did all of this to protect your secret, a secret that no one would really care about!" Grandma was nearly shouting and I tried to put my hand on her arm to quiet her down, but she just shook it off.

"No one would care about?" Mitzie scoffed. "I care about it! And I'm sure the mayor would've cared about it. Certainly his wife would have!"

"So that's why you left town," Grandma said, pulling out another paper from the box and opening it. "The mayor paid you off after he found out you were pregnant."

Mitzie's face turned cold. "You don't understand," she said. "He gave me a lot of money to raise my son somewhere else. But our agreement was that if anyone ever found out, I'd have to pay it all back. There's no way I can afford to return that money."

Grandma looked at the paper she held in her hands and her eyes bugged out a little. "That's a lot of money."

"It was!" Mitzie snatched the paper from Grandma. "It was enough that I could raise him comfortably."

"So let me guess," Grandma said, shaking the box a little. "When you first came to town and you stopped by my shop, you were looking for this box. When you couldn't find it, you burned it down."

"My stupid brother started giving her things away before she even died!" Tears filled Mitzie's eyes. "My mother was the only one who knew the truth. I gave her the papers before I left town all those years ago just in case…in case something ever happened to me and it was suspicious. I wanted someone else to know the truth. She put them in that box and it stayed on her dresser for twenty years. And then Andrew decided to take a bunch of her things to your shop!"

Mitzie started crying.

"Why didn't you just ask me for them?" Grandma asked, kindness returning to her voice. "You know I would've given it all back to you."

"I didn't want to draw attention to them and you'd look inside."

"So you burned down my shop," Grandma said flatly. Then her eyes lit up. "And let me guess, you're also the person behind all the bills from the city that Detective Owen found that day."

Mitzie wiped the tears from her eyes and stood up straight. "You can't prove that."

"You broke into city hall and somehow you did

something to my account so it looked like I owed the city a bunch of money."

Mitzie's face took a prideful look. "Not much has changed in twenty years," she said. "I expected it to take a bit of time for me to break into their system, but it was the same system I used twenty years ago."

"I have a question," I said from behind Grandma Dean. "You set the fire and forged city documents to make it look like Grandma was delinquent… Did you also steal her things from her storage shed?"

"I went in to visit Bev one day and she told me you were opening another shop. She mentioned you had a storage unit where you kept your overflow and that you were going to use it to open your shop. I panicked, thinking what if the boxes had been in there the whole time and not in your first shop. I went over there and the unit's door was wide open. I threw what was in there in my car and when that box wasn't there, I came here last night and there it was! In Perry's hand!"

I shuddered. Poor Perry. I didn't know what he was doing in Grandma's shop in the middle of the night, but whatever it was, he didn't deserve to die because of it.

"How did you get him to write the note," Grandma asked quietly. "The police said it was in his own handwriting."

Mitzie laughed. "I told him to. I gave him a piece of paper and a pen and told him exactly what to say. He didn't even question me! Can you believe that? He just did what he was told."

I was so angry in that moment that I wanted to beat her senseless. Grandma must have had the same thought because within seconds, she had lunged at Mitzie and knocked her down. The gun flew out of her hand and skidded across the floor. I picked it up and held it out, ready to shoot it if I had to. But Grandma and Mitzie were tangled up and I wasn't sure I could hit Mitzie and not Grandma.

A sound at the door startled me and I aimed the gun in that direction.

"Put that down," Detective Owen shouted at me as he reached down and grabbed Mitzie by the back of the head, pulling her off Grandma and onto her feet.

Both women were bleeding and out of breath. A quick look at them showed that Grandma was clearly the winner in that battle—coming out of it with a few scratches and a busted lip compared with Mitzie's very broken nose.

Officer Tomlin, a portly fellow with a genuine smile, came over and took the gun from me. "It's okay now," he said gently. "You're safe."

I turned to Grandma, threw my arms around her, and squeezed her tiny frame.

She gasped for air. "I survived Mitzie only to be killed by my own granddaughter."

I let go. "You called me your granddaughter!" I exclaimed.

"It's because no one is in here listening."

She was right. Detective Owen had taken Mitzie outside and Officer Tomlin had followed. I didn't care if no one heard. I heard it.

"I think we should finish our little vacation," Grandma said, pulling me close. "I think you and I deserve it."

"You won't make me get a spray tan, will you?" I asked as we walked out.

"It's either that or a bikini wax."

"I'll choose the spray tan."

"I had a feeling you would."

EPILOGUE

WHEN WE RETURNED from our trip to the spa a few days later, I scooped up Catalie Portman and took her to my room. I needed someone to talk to for a minute and over the last few weeks, I had come to trust her with my deepest darkest secrets.

On my way back to my room, Grandma called for me from the couch where she was reading the mail.

"Hey," she said as I walked in. "I was thinking that maybe you and I should open a business together, now that I have the keys back to my first shop. It will take a few weeks to get Joe's brother in there to clean it all up, but I think we can turn it into something fabulous."

"I don't know," I said, trying to word things in a way that wouldn't hurt her feelings. "I think I've had enough excitement for a while. I think I might head back home and start dealing with the messes I've made there."

Grandma's face fell and I knew she was disappointed. "All right," she said. "I can understand that. Before you go to your room, I have something for you."

She dug in her purse and pulled out a box.

"What is it?" I asked, setting down the cat. I sat down next to Grandma Dean on the couch.

"It's a new phone." She handed it to me. "It's all set up and ready to go. I even made accounts for you on all the social media sites."

She pulled up her favorite one and showed me how it worked. "If you want to search for someone, just hit that little magnifying glass at the top and type in their name. It's as easy as that!"

"Thank you," I said, taking the phone. "Not just for this, but for opening your home to me."

Grandma Dean smiled. "You've come a long way in just a few weeks, but I'm not done with you yet." Her eyes softened and turned glassy. "You're welcome to come back any time and we'll pick back up right where we left off."

I laughed. "Me with a blotchy, fading spray tan and you with two stitches in your lip?"

Grandma Dean laughed with me. "Well, you can't say your time in Florida wasn't exciting!"

I went to my room and Catalie Portman followed me. I climbed under the covers and Catalie snuggled next to me. I held the new phone in my hand. I tried to resist the urge to look up everyone I knew on the site

Grandma Dean had shown me, but the temptation was too strong. I clicked on the app and it instantly opened. I typed in my mom's name, Marilyn Parker. To my surprise, her picture popped up. I read through some of her posts and laughed. Suddenly, and for the first time since I'd left home, I missed her.

I typed in my sister's name, Amber Parker Cooper. There she was, smiling in the picture while her boys climbed all over her.

My finger hovered over the magnifying glass on the screen for a minute before I typed in Bo's name. My heart flooded with emotion as I stared at his profile picture when it came up. "I'm coming home," I whispered to him.

I scrolled down to see if he had posted anything about missing me and suddenly it felt like my heart stopped beating. I couldn't believe what I was seeing. There, in the middle of his page, was a picture with him and Darcy McGee. She had her arm around him and it looked like they were laughing. I recognized their surroundings immediately. They were at the Wooden Pickle bar in our hometown.

I turned off the phone and threw it at the end of the bed. He didn't wait for me like he said he would. I laid down and put my head next to Catalie's as I fought back tears. Could I blame him, though? I hadn't exactly stayed away from the opposite sex while I had been here. I had fallen for Joe and had briefly considered falling for Owen, until he ticked me off.

I rolled onto my back and stared at the ceiling for a minute. Then I got out of bed and walked into the living room.

"I've been thinking," I said to Grandma Dean. "I think we should turn your old shop into a clothing store. We could call it the Chic Boutique."

Grandma looked at me, her face lighting up and a smile overtaking her face. "I love it! And we can have an entire clothing line just for cats!"

It wasn't exactly what I was picturing, but it would work.

"Perfect," I said to her. "On to our next adventure!"

THANK YOU!

Thanks for reading *Up in Smoke*. I have a lot of fun writing the Glock Grannies books and I hope you have fun reading them!

If you enjoyed this book, or even if you didn't, it would be awesome if you left a review for me on Amazon and/or Goodreads. That will really help me tell others about the book because Amazon shares books that have a lot of reviews with more people.

The next book in the Glock Grannies Cozy Mystery series is called *The Root of All Evil*. We're talking about Money and it is not only the root of all evil, it's also the root of a murder mystery.

. . .

I have included a preview from another book that I think you will like. It is a preview of *A Pie to Die For* by Stacey Alabaster - it's part of the popular Bakery Detectives Cozy Mystery series. I really hope you like the sample. If you do, the book is available on Amazon.

Lastly, if you would like to know about future cozy mysteries by me and the other authors at Fairfield Publishing, make sure to sign up for our Cozy Mystery Newsletter. We will send you our FREE Cozy Mystery Starter Library just for signing up. All the details are on the next page.

FAIRFIELD COZY MYSTERY NEWSLETTER

Make sure you sign up for the Fairfield Cozy Mystery Newsletter so you can keep up with our latest releases. When you sign up, **we will send you our FREE Cozy Mystery Starter Library!**

FairfieldPublishing.com/cozy-newsletter/

PREVIEW: A PIE TO DIE FOR

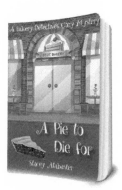

"But you don't understand, I use only the finest, organic ingredients." My voice was high-pitched as I pleaded my case to the policeman. Oh, this was just like an episode of Criminal Point. Hey, I wondered who the killer turned out to be. I shook my head. That's not important, Rachael, I scolded myself. *What's important*

is getting yourself off this murder charge. Still, I hoped Pippa had recorded the ending of the episode.

I tried to steady my breathing as Jackson—Detective Whitaker—entered the room and threw a folder on the table, before studying the contents as though he was cramming for a test he had to take the next day. He rubbed his temples and frowned.

Is he even going to make eye contact with me? Is he just going to completely ignore the interaction we had at the fair? Pretend it never even happened.

"Jackson..." I started, before I was met with a steely glare. "Detective. Surely you can't think I had anything to do with this?"

Jackson looked up at me slowly. "Had you ever had any contact with Mrs. Batters before today?"

I shifted in my seat. "Yes," I had to admit. "I knew her a little from the store. She was always quite antagonistic towards me, but I'd never try to kill her!"

"Witnesses near the scene said that you two had an argument." He gave me that same steely glare. Where was the charming, flirty, sweet guy I'd meet earlier? He was now buried beneath a suit and a huge attitude.

"Well...it wasn't an argument...she was just...winding me up, like she always does."

Jackson shot me a sharp look. "So, she was annoying you? Was she making you angry?"

"Well... Well..." I tripped over my words. He was now making me nervous for an entirely different reason than he had earlier. Those butterflies were back, but now they felt like daggers.

Come on, Rach. Everyone knows that the first suspect in Criminal Point is not the one that actually did it.

But how many people had Jackson already interviewed? Maybe he was saving me for last. Gosh, maybe my cherry pie had actually killed the woman!

"Answer the question please, Miss Robinson."

"Not angry, no. I was just frustrated."

"Frustrated?" A smile curled at his lips before he pounced. "Frustrated with Mrs. Batters?"

"No! The situation. Come on—you were there!" I tried to appeal to his sympathies, but he remained a brick wall.

"It doesn't matter whether I was there or not. That is entirely besides the point." He said the words a little too forcefully.

I swallowed. "I couldn't get any customers to try my cakes, and Bakermatic was luring everyone away with their free samples." I stopped as my brows shot up involuntarily. "Jackson! Sorry, Detective. Mrs. Batters ate at Bakermatic as well!"

My words came out in a stream of breathless blabber as I raced to get them out. "Bakermatic must be to blame! They cut corners, they use cheap ingredients. Oh, and I know how much Mrs. Batters loved their food! She was always eating there. Believe me, she made that very clear to me."

Jackson sat back and folded his arms across his chest. "Don't try to solve this case for us."

I sealed my lips. *Looks like I might have to at this rate.*

"We are investigating every place Mrs. Batters ate today. You don't need to worry about that."

I leaned forward and banged my palm on the table. "But I do need to worry about it! This is my job, my livelihood…my life on the line. If people think I am to blame, that will be the final nail in my bakery's coffin!" Oh, what a day. And I'd thought it was bad enough that I hadn't gotten any customers at my stand. Now I was being accused of killing a woman!

I could have sworn I saw a flicker of sympathy finally crawl across Jackson's face. He stood up and readjusted his tie, but he still refused to make full eye contact. "You're free to go, Miss Robinson," he said gently. There was that tone from earlier, finally. He seemed recognizable as a human at long last.

"Really?"

He nodded. "For the moment. But we might have some more questions for you later, so don't leave town."

I tried to make eye contact with him as I left, squirreling out from underneath his arm as he held the door open for me, but he just kept staring at the floor.

Did that mean he wasn't coming back to my bakery after all?

PIPPA WAS STILL WAITING for me when I returned home later that evening. There was a chill in the air, which meant that I headed straight for a blanket and the fireplace when I finally crawled in through the door. Pippa shot me a sympathetic look as I curled up and crumbled in front of the flames. *How had today gone so wrong, so quickly?*

"I recorded the last part of the show," Pippa said softly. "If you're up for watching it."

I groaned and lay on the carpet, my back straight against the floor like I was a little kid. "I don't think I can stomach it after what I just went through. Can you believe it? Accusing ME of killing Mrs. Batters? When I *know* that Bakermatic is to blame. I mean, Pippa, they must be! But this detective wouldn't even listen to me when I was trying to explain Bakermatic's dodgy practices to him."

Pippa leaned forward and took the lid off a pot, the smell of the brew hitting my nose. "Pippa, what is that?"

She grinned and stirred it, which only made the smell worse. I leaned back and covered my nose. "Thought it might be a bit heavy for you. I basically took every herb, tea, and spice that you had in your cabinet and came up with this! I call it 'Pippa's Delight'!"

"Yeah well, it doesn't sound too delightful." I sat up and scrunched up my nose. "Oh, what the heck—pour me a cup."

"Are you sure?" Pippa asked with a cheeky grin.

"Go on. I'll be brave."

I braced myself as the brown liquid hit the white mug.

It was as disgusting as I had imagined, but at least it made me laugh when the pungent concoction hit my tongue. Pippa always had a way of cheering me up. If it wasn't her unusual concoctions, or her ever changing hair color—red this week but pink the last, and purple a week before that—then it was her never-ending array of careers and job changes that entertained me and kept me on my toes. When you're trying to run your own business, forced to be responsible day in and day out, you have to live vicariously through some of your more free-spirited friends. And Pippa was definitely that: free-spirited.

"Hey!" I said suddenly, as an idea began to brew in my brain. I didn't know if it was the tea that suddenly brought all my senses to life or what it was, but I found myself slamming my mug on the table with new found enthusiasm. "Pippa, have you got a job at the moment?" I could never keep up with Pippa's present state of employment.

She shrugged as she kicked her feet up and lay back on the sofa. "Not really! I mean, I've got a couple of things in the works. Why's that?"

I pondered for a moment. "Pippa, if you could get a job at Bakermatic, you could see first hand what they're up to!" My voice was a rush of excitement as I clapped my hands together. "You would get to find out the ways they cut corners, the bad ingredients they use, and, if you were really lucky, you might even overhear someone say something about Mrs. Batters!"

A gleam appeared in Pippa's green eyes. "Well, I do need a job, especially after today."

I raced on. "Yes! And you've got plenty of experience working in cafes."

"Yeah. I've worked in hundreds of places." She took a sip of the tea and managed to swallow it. She actually seemed to enjoy it.

"I know you've got a lot of experience. You're sure to get the job. They're always looking for part-timers." Unfortunately, Bakermatic was planning on expanding the storefront even further, and that meant they were looking for even more employees to fill their big yellow store. "Pippa, this is the perfect plan! We'll get you an application first thing in the morning. Then you can start investigating!"

Pippa raised her eyebrows. "Investigating?"

I nodded and lay my head back down on the carpet. "Criminal Point—Belldale Style! Bakery Investigation Unit! I will investigate and do what I can from my end as well! Perhaps I could talk to people from all the other food stalls! Oh, Pippa, we're going to make a crack team of detectives!"

"The Bakery Detectives!"

We both started giggling but, as the full weight of the day's events started to pile up on me, I felt my stomach tighten. It might seem fun to send Pippa in to spy on Bakermatic, but this was serious. My bakery, my livelihood, and even my own freedom depended on it.

THANKS FOR READING a sample of *A Pie to Die For*. I really hope you liked it.

YOU CAN GET it for free by signing up for our newsletter.

FairfieldPublishing.com/cozy-newsletter/